CUPID'S WEB

CUPID'S WEB

•

Carolyn Hughey

AVALON BOOKS
NEW YORK

Published by Thomas Bouregy & Co., Inc.
160 Madison Avenue, New York, NY 10016

Library of Congress Cataloging-in-Publication Data

Hughey, Carolyn.
  Cupid's web / Carolyn Hughey.
      p.   cm.
  ISBN 978-0-8034-9854-9 (acid-free paper)   1. Women in
marketing—Fiction.   2. New York (N.Y.)—Fiction.   I. Title.

PS3608.U3769C87   2007
813'.6—dc22

                                        2007016630

PRINTED IN THE UNITED STATES OF AMERICA
ON ACID-FREE PAPER
BY HADDON CRAFTSMEN, BLOOMSBURG, PENNSYLVANIA

To Mom, Johanna, and Kim
You're the best!

I owe a huge thanks to so many wonderful people who willingly held my hand during the creation of *Cupid's Web*.

To Deb Dufel, who encouraged me to write the book of my heart and pushed me into joining RWA. I couldn't have made a better decision. Your persistence led the way. Thank you.

To my mother-in-law, June Hughey, who told me I could write.

To my critique buddies Ardath Albee, Sheila Rae Mohs, Nan Strebeck, Mona Risk and Marlene Urso. I can't tell you how much I've appreciated the time and energy you extended on my behalf. It has been invaluable to me.

To Joel Hochberg, who has generously offered his skillful knowledge. Thanks for leading the way.

To Erin Cartwright Niumata at Avalon Books, who picked up my manuscript and read it.

And lastly, to Bob, my wonderful husband, who has always believed in me. Your support and encouragement have meant the world to me. Thank you for allowing me to fulfill another one of my dreams.

Chapter One

"**L**ook out! New York City, here I come!" I exclaimed enthusiastically, stepping off the train onto the platform. I walked briskly through Penn Station's busy terminal and out onto the crowded sidewalk. The hustle bustle of the crowd surrounding me was invigorating. A combination of cheap perfume and stale cigarette smoke permeated the air as people marched by in a robotic fashion.

I passed a coffee shop and decided to stop and buy something chocolate to celebrate. Today marked a new beginning, a new life, a new job—a "free to be me" day. A Cassie Pirelli Independence Day, away from a meddling mother who drove me crazy with her well-meaning intentions.

A long line of customers extended out to the sidewalk.

I stepped up behind a small-framed woman with big hair. I was bursting with excitement about my new-found freedom. My giddiness got the best of me, and all I could think about was sharing my good news. I didn't care who I told, but I was going to tell someone. I tapped little Ms. Big Hair on the shoulder.

"Hey, today is my first day of independence. Yeah, this is it." I giggled with excitement. "As soon as the money starts coming in from my new job at Merrill Finance Corporation, I'll be moving here too."

The woman looked over her shoulder to see who was touching her, gave me a dirty look, then turned back without a word. I didn't care. I was going to share my good news regardless, so I spoke to the back of her head.

"Yep," I said with confidence, "I'm going to be planning events, talking to customers, and writing sales presentations for the vice president of marketing."

The woman turned around again, this time with a disdainful look on her face. In a sarcastic, native New York accent, she said, "Yeah, and I just lowered my cholesterol."

And there you have it. My fifteen minutes of fame right down the dumper.

Thoughts of calling her an old grump crossed my mind, but I figured she already knew that. The line was moving more slowly than I'd hoped, so I decided to forego the celebratory chocolate. Besides, little Ms. Big Hair wasn't much fun to be around, and I wasn't going to let anyone rain on my parade—not today. But really, would it have killed little Miss Big Hair to listen to me? Sheesh.

I continued on my journey and decided to let go of negative thoughts. After all, I was going to be working for a big shot now, and acting professional was paramount. My heart skipped a beat as I thought about how excited I was to be in the city that never sleeps. My thoughts drifted to meeting my new boss for the first time. I was hoping I was going to like him. Better yet, that he was going to like me. I felt liberated, knowing I'd taken the first step toward my independence. Excitement reeled inside me, and I thought about how much fun my best friend, Megan O'Malley, and I were going to have finding a new apartment in this glorious city. I'd dreamed of this day since I was a child, after listening to Uncle Nicky's tales about life in the Big Apple.

The street sign said PARK AVENUE, and I knew I was but a short distance away. I grinned with excitement, throwing my arms into the air and shouting, "Wahoo!"

So much for professionalism. I couldn't seem to help myself.

Two blocks later I stopped on a corner and waited for the traffic light to change. When it did, I jogged across the street and up the steps into my new office building, then headed down the corridor to the elevators.

A foxy-looking guy stood waiting patiently for one to arrive. The hunk wore a pinstriped suit with a red power tie. He held a briefcase in one hand and a partially open newspaper in the other. He looked up from his paper for a second when I approached him and smiled.

"Good morning," I said with effervescence. Foxy Guy nodded. I concluded that he was an up-and-coming executive. But he was just too hot for words, and I was having a hard time taking my eyes off his I-work-out-every-day body.

I continued to peek at him out of the corner of my eye. His reddish brown wavy hair and perfectly shaped face gave off a bronzed glow as if from summer sunshine. He looked up from his newspaper again. He must have sensed I was giving him the sidelong glance, because the corners of his mouth curled into a smile. He lowered his head and resumed reading. I avoided eye contact. I was embarrassed he'd caught me checking him out.

I began to daydream about being on some deserted island with this godlike creature, unaware an elevator had arrived. I quickly snapped to attention when I heard him speak.

"Are you getting in?" he said, already inside and holding the door open with one foot.

"Oh. Yes. Thanks." The masculine scent of his aftershave penetrated my nostrils as I breezed past him. Standing next to him made my heart do flip-flops.

Hmm, if this guy is any indication of who works in this place . . . mmm, nice. No wedding band on that left hand, either.

What am I doing, for God's sake? It's only been a month since I broke my engagement. . . . But then, I never said I didn't like men—I just don't want to be married to one. Not yet. Unlike many, I want to get my career—and my independence—on track first.

"What floor?" he asked.

"Twenty please."

"I'm headed in that direction too."

He turned his attention back to his paper. The door closed, and we started to rise. Without warning, the elevator sputtered and jerked to a halt. I lost my balance and fell into Foxy Guy, sending my briefcase smack into his knee. His newspaper fell from his hand and scattered as his briefcase hit the floor with a thud.

He grimaced with pain from the force of the impact but managed to steady me with one hand while clutching his knee with the other.

"I am so sorry. Are you okay?"

"Yeah, I guess." His handsome face was contorted with pain. "I'm just coming back to work after recuperating from knee surgery."

"Oh, no!" I pointed to the knee I'd just walloped. "Is that the one?"

He nodded and bent over to massage it. Helpless, I looked on with embarrassment, knowing his discomfort was my fault. But I didn't think saying something would make it any better.

I cringed and chastised myself. *Now you've done it, Cass. Yikes! Ooh, please tell me I didn't just do that.*

Foxy Guy stood upright, leaned against a wall, and stretched his leg out in front of him, then bent it behind a few times.

I watched. "Does that help?"

"A little." He grimaced. "I need to sit down to get the weight off my knee."

"That's probably a good idea," I said, getting down on my knees to scoop up his newspaper. I reassembled it and handed it back to him.

"Thank you."

He noticed the concerned look on my face.

"I'll be fine. Stop worrying."

"Does sitting make it feel any better?"

"It'll be okay."

He pointed to a silver panel on the wall. "If you'll hand me the phone behind that panel, I'll call maintenance."

I did as he asked and opened the small door containing the telephone and handed it to him.

"Steve?" he said as he smiled faintly into the receiver. "Yes, it is. It certainly has been a long time—six weeks to be exact." He nodded as if Steve was standing in front of him.

I watched him handle the situation while he continued answering ol' Steve's questions.

"I'm getting better all the time, thanks. The elevator is at a standstill. Again. We're between floors somewhere, but the number lights went out, so I'm not sure where." He smiled into the phone. "I thought you guys fixed this problem. I realize that, but it seems worse today than it was before. Okay, thanks. Yeah, it's nice to be back."

When he finished, he handed me the phone to put back into its enclosure. The look on my face must have told him what I was thinking.

"Maintenance said it will be fixed as soon as they can," he reassured me.

"What, exactly, does that mean?"

He snickered. "It means as soon as they can."

He looked down at his paper and resumed reading. The silence was driving me crazy, so I began to pace. I strained to hear voices or a noise, anything that would indicate the maintenance crew was working to fix the problem, but the only sound I heard was Foxy Guy's breathing and the rustle of his newspaper. I ultimately concluded that no one was working on the elevator. Relying on intestinal fortitude was no longer an option, and I blurted out in anguish, "Shoot! This is just what I need this morning. I'm going to be late for my first day on the job."

I increased the speed of my pacing—a pretty difficult task in a four-by-six box, especially with his outstretched legs taking up half the space.

"Get used to it. This happens frequently."

"So"—I checked my watch—"he said a few minutes, huh?"

"No. He said he'd get to it as soon as he could." He held up a hand as if swearing on the Bible. "But I promise, you'll even have enough time to powder your nose before you meet your new boss." He went back to his paper.

"I hope Mr. Brixler won't be upset with me if I'm late."

He looked up from his paper and smiled. In a firm but friendly voice he said, "Don't worry. You're not going to be late."

"I haven't met him yet, and I'm nervous."

"You think?" He grinned and lowered his head, giving his newspaper top billing.

"I'm really excited about this job, but not knowing anything about him, I'm feeling a bit apprehensive, wondering what I'm getting myself into. The man who conducted the interview for Mr. Brixler was very nice, and I wouldn't mind working for him, but . . ."

His brows knitted together in question. "If you had so many concerns, why did you take the job?"

"You know what?" I shrugged. "I really wanted to work at Merrill."

He grinned. "Then what are you so nervous about?"

"Well, if Mr. Garrett was the one who told him to hire me, maybe he won't like me. And if he doesn't like me, then he'll fire me. And if I get fired, I won't be able to advance in the business, and if I don't advance, I can't prove to Mom . . ." I stopped talking and started to giggle. The expression on his face was priceless.

"Gee, listen to me ramble on. I guess I am wound up pretty tight."

He shook his head from side to side, a grin on his face, and went back to reading the paper again. I really wanted to take that paper of his and rip it to shreds, but I didn't need this stranger to witness any more of my erratic behavior than he'd already seen.

Man, I need to get a grip. I'm doing an outstanding job in the first-impressions department, aren't I? Not.

A sudden grinding noise alerted us that the elevator was about to move, and we began to rise. I released a sigh of relief. The remainder of the trip was made in silence. I watched the numbers light up as we passed each floor. When we reached the twentieth, the doors opened, and I leaned against them to prevent them from closing on the guy I'd crippled. He rolled over to kneel on his good knee and pulled himself up. I allowed him to exit first. After all, that was the least I could do.

He pointed to the right. "The women's restroom is that way."

"Thanks."

I smiled and waved, watching him limp down the hall in the opposite direction. I really felt bad, knowing I was the one who'd hurt him. Halfway down the hall he turned back to call to me, "Good luck. I hope you'll be very happy here at Merrill."

I smiled back at him. "Thank you. By the way, what did you say your name . . ." My voice trailed off as I heard a door close, and he was gone.

Chapter Two

"**I**'m such a moron!" I snapped my fingers. "I can't believe I didn't ask his name." I shook my head from side to side, annoyed at my stupidity. I mulled over the prospects of meeting him again and walked to the ladies' room.

"Forget it, sunshine," I continued out loud. "I don't think Mr. Foxy Guy would be interested in sharing the same space with you again."

I began to primp in front of the mirror—you know, checking the makeup, smoothing my skirt, trying to iron out the wrinkles from my long train ride. I wanted to make a good first impression and hoped the new guy thought I was worth the hiring.

A few minutes later I was refreshed—well, sort of— and ready to take on the world, eager to meet the new boss. Unfortunately, that refreshed feeling lasted, like, a nanosecond, and my heart resumed its accelerated rate of anxiety as I neared the reception area. I inhaled and exhaled a few times to relieve the tension. My hands nervously fiddled with my skirt.

I entered the reception area and walked up to Mr. Brixler's secretary, who sat staring at her computer. I was happy to see the same secretary still working for the company. But, hey, it had only been two weeks since my interview, so I guess that wasn't a fair assessment. But a good sign, for sure.

She stood to greet me. "Good morning, Cassie. Welcome to the Merrill Finance Company."

"Thanks, Victoria."

She walked out from behind her desk. She was a very attractive woman, tall and slender with short, trendy blond hair, and dressed as though she'd just stepped off the cover of *Elle* magazine. I recognized her navy tailored suit as a Versace and immediately became self-conscious, wondering if anyone would recognize my Armani knockoff.

I extended my right hand. "It's nice to be here."

I gave the area a quick scan. I hadn't really noticed how classy the office was during my last visit. I'd been disappointed I wasn't being interviewed by Mr. Brixler. They said he was out, but I wondered why no one had called to cancel the meeting or to reschedule.

A floral scent drew my attention. To the right of Victoria's desk was a lava rock wall with water running down into a trough adorned with colorful flowers. The reception area was decorated in soft hues of lavender and beige with blue accents. Plants were scattered around, and the soothing trickle of water and soft music playing in the background created a calming and comfortable atmosphere. That was good thing. I needed some calm.

Victoria pointed to a door to her left. "Mr. Brixler is waiting for you."

"I can't wait to finally meet him."

She looked at me quizzically. "Oh, that's right. I'd forgotten. The day you interviewed, Ryan Garrett was covering for him. Barry was out for a few weeks." She smiled reassuringly. "He's a wonderful boss." She nodded in the direction of his door. "Go ahead. Don't keep him waiting."

I mustered up a weak smile. The phone started to ring, and she walked quickly toward her desk. "I'm looking forward to working with you."

"Me too, thanks."

I knocked on the office door and entered when I heard his muffled voice. My feet sank deeply into thick beige plush carpeting. A familiar scent filled the room. I closed the door and turned around to meet my new boss for the first time.

Sheer panic enveloped my entire body, and I quickly averted my eyes. My lips went numb, and I began to hyperventilate. I struggled to speak, but a large knot formed in my throat, blocking passage of any sound.

Nothing came out—nothing, nada. My legs felt like posts as thoughts raced through my mind at record speed. I forced myself to look at him—my new boss— the man sitting with one leg propped up on a pillow, an ice bag covering the knee.

Oh. My. God.

"Cassie? Are you okay?"

I think I nodded, but I'm not sure.

"I'm Barry Brixler."

No kidding. I thought. *Nice time to tell me.*

He motioned to a chair tucked under a small conference table at one end of the room. "Please, pull up a chair and sit." He leaned forward from the waist and extended his right hand in greeting, engulfing my limp, sweaty palm, which undoubtedly reminded him of a dead fish.

"Well," I said in a state of self-conscious distress. "What an awkward moment. So much for first impressions, huh?"

With a slight grin on his face, he said, "Don't give it another thought. It wasn't your fault the elevator threw you off balance. I apologize for not introducing myself earlier. It was my first day back at the office. I'd actually forgotten you were starting today and didn't remember until you mentioned your concern about being late. I could see you were embarrassed and nervous, and I just didn't have the heart to tell you. I figured you'd learn my identity soon enough."

I nodded but remained silent, a tight knot in my

throat making me feel as if I had a noose around my neck. I could feel the heat rushing to my cheeks. I decided to keep my mouth shut for fear I'd say something dumb. *Yeah, like that hasn't happened before.*

He began telling me about the role I would play in the organization. I couldn't focus on anything except what had happened.

He stopped talking and stared at me. "You look confused," he said with a frown. "Are you? You know, if you have anything you want to ask, just jump in at any time."

I cleared my throat and searched to find the right words. In a squeaky, apologetic voice, I said, "Um, I . . . uh . . . I am so sorry, Mr. Brixler."

He relaxed his facial muscles and smiled. "Please stop apologizing."

The tenseness of the moment faded somewhat.

"Are you ready to get started?" he asked.

"Yes."

"Good. Let's go over a few things before I have to rush off to a meeting. After I leave, Victoria will take you around to meet the staff. First matter of business, though—please call me Barry. After all, we're already pretty good friends now, aren't we?" he teased.

"I guess there's no chance I'm ever going to live this one down, is there?"

"No, I'm afraid not." He stifled a soft chuckle.

"Okay, Mr. Brixler—I mean, Barry." *I can't believe this man is my boss.*

My thoughts came to a screeching halt when he sat

silently, staring at me, as though waiting for me to say something.

"What?" tripped off the tip of my tongue.

We both laughed at my abrupt response. "Cassie, are you all right? This is the second time you've had that strange look on your face." He stared at me for a second. "Would you like a cup of coffee?"

"Actually, I'd love one. Thank you for asking."

He pointed in the direction of a circular bar tucked in a corner. Leather-covered stools surrounded its carved mahogany. "I'm afraid you'll have to help yourself. I'd like to keep this ice on my knee to minimize swelling."

"Certainly," I mumbled. "Can I get you a cup?"

"No thanks."

His office was beautifully appointed. A tall tree stood in a corner next to a huge window that looked out over an array of tall buildings. At the other end of the office an entire wall was dedicated to bookshelves. A rolling ladder attached to a rail offered easy access to any volume. In the opposite corner a spiral staircase supported a loft area furnished with a burgundy leather sofa and chairs.

A grin covered his face. "It really is nice meeting you, Cassie. I think you'll complement our group very nicely."

"Thank you. I think you're very nice too," I said awkwardly.

"You're not just trying to flatter me, are you?" he asked.

I shook my head and opened my eyes wide with surprise. "Oh, no, sir, I'm not."

He stood and limped to his desk to buzz the intercom. When Victoria entered, he said, "Please show Cassie to her office, let her meet the staff, and do whatever else needs doing for new employees. I have to run." He checked his watch and spoke directly to me. "I have to get out of here. I have a meeting with our CEO in a few minutes." He made his way to the door, removed the cane that stood upright in an umbrella stand, and began to leave. Halfway out, he turned to look at me. "I'll see you later, okay?"

"That's fine, thanks," I responded, still frazzled. Once he was out of sight, I released a deep sigh of relief.

A sympathetic expression crossed Victoria's face. "Tough morning, huh?"

"I'll say. Do you know what happened?"

"Yes. And I told him he should have told you who he was. At times he can be a bit of a jokester, but trust me, you'll get used to it. He's very good to his employees."

"But I whacked him in the knee! The bad one!"

"Well, he limped in this morning and told me he'd definitely selected the right person for the job."

"I am so relieved to hear that. Thank you for telling me."

"Okay, shall we take a stroll so I can introduce you to some of the staff?"

"Yes, I'd like that."

We headed down the hall.

After meeting a lot of people, we walked back to the executive area and into my new office. Imagine my surprise when we entered a room totally devoid of any personality whatsoever. There was a bookcase filled with binders, two straight back chairs upholstered with a floral print, and a large desk and leather chair.

I don't know what I was expecting. Well, I do know what I was expecting, but I guess I'll just have to wait until I get a promotion. In the meantime, being in the executive area was reason enough to celebrate. A few pictures, some green plants, and various trinkets would make the room homier. After all, I was going to be spending a lot of time here.

I waltzed around and squealed with delight when I noticed I actually had a window. "Wow," I said, pointing at it.

Victoria laughed. "Uh, Cass, I think you should take a look out first."

I eagerly rushed to see the view. That "view" was of another, equally sterile office. Turning my head in either direction made no difference. I gave it one more shot and looked down, wondering if I'd be able to see anything from the twentieth floor. That turned out to be a moot issue as well. But, hey, that's life.

I turned away from the window. "At least I have daylight coming through.

"There you go," Victoria said. "I knew you'd find a

positive in there somewhere. Okay, I need to get back to my desk and get some work done." She turned to leave. "Buzz me if you have any questions."

"Thank you. I'll catch up with you later."

She left, and I began looking through the files in my desk drawers to become familiar with how my predecessor had handled the job. When I finished with the files, I walked to the bookcase to look through the binders. Each contained detailed information about the conferences that were scheduled and copies of Barry's previous marketing presentations.

I sat down in the chair behind my desk. I couldn't wait to sit with my feet up on the desk, the way all the hotshot executives do. Because I was wearing a skirt, I checked to see that the door was closed. I slipped out of my shoes and put my feet up, rolled from side to side to adjust my skirt to be sure it provided adequate coverage, just in case someone walked in, then crossed my ankles. I leaned back, my hands clasped behind my head, taking in the sweet satisfaction of the moment.

"Wow," I said aloud, looking around the room, "this is my very own office. If my friends could only see me now."

I was happy to be alone. I needed time to catch my breath. I rested my head against the cushion of my leather chair and began to relive the events of the morning. I pictured Mr. Brixler apologizing for not identifying himself on the elevator. Chuckling, I thought about the challenges I'd face by working for such a sexy, good-looking man. Just the thought brought back the giddiness I'd felt at Penn Station.

I knew I was acting like an infatuated schoolgirl, but the new boss wasn't what I'd expected. I finally concluded that there wasn't any good reason not to enjoy the scenery. I was quickly jolted back to reality when my cell phone rang.

"Hello?" I scrunched up my face when I recognized the familiar voice at the other end. It was my mother. I'd been so busy, I'd forgotten to call and cancel our lunch. I knew she wasn't going to be happy with me, but that wasn't anything new.

"Cassie, where are you?" she demanded.

"Ooh, Mom, I'm sorry I didn't call you." I squirmed in my seat. "I'm still at work," I said, gritting my teeth.

"Everyone is sitting around the table waiting for you," she announced.

I come from one of those close-knit Italian families. All the relatives work in the same area and live about a block from one another. Due to the proximity, the aunts and uncles all congregate at Mom's for lunch. Up until now that included me. But I used to work at a law firm in Nutley. Mom didn't know I'd taken this job in New York. I'd decided to tell her after the fact, at Sunday's "Family Fest," with the rest of the relatives around for support.

"I'm up to my eyeballs in work, so please don't hold lunch for me. And tell everyone I'm sorry I didn't call sooner."

"So what are *you* going to eat, then?" she asked.

"Oh, I'll grab something from the café on the corner."

"Why don't I bring something over to your office?"

My heart began racing. "No! I—I mean, no thanks. Actually, I just remembered that one of the girls brought in some stew she made last night for us. I'll eat that."

"So why didn't you just say that to begin with? You didn't have to lie about being too busy to join us."

"I wasn't lying. I really am very busy. Actually, I'm working on a big assignment, so you might as well count me out for the rest of the week too."

The reason I hadn't told Mom about my new job beforehand was because she's a bit of a drama queen who does not like losing control of her family. Namely me, her only child. I knew once she heard the news, she'd bring in the heavy artillery. And I was afraid I'd get cold feet and turn down the job offer of a lifetime. I figured it was better to wait until Sunday. Megan would be there to cheer me on, and I'd already be ensconced in my new position, so there'd be no fear of Mom's talking me out of it.

When my friends and I compared notes, we agreed that our mothers must all belong to some secret Italian Mamas' Society, pledging to drive their daughters insane by upholding the Code of Guilt.

"Aw, I'm so disappointed," she said. I could almost see her pouting. "I was looking forward to having lunch with you today. I miss you so much when you're not here."

Here it comes.

"It's not going to be the same without you."

Bingo!

My conversation was interrupted when the door to my office opened with a soft whoosh of air and Barry Brixler entered. His eyebrows arched when he noticed my feet up on the desk, causing his mouth to curl into a crooked smile. My immediate reaction was to snap to attention with my feet under the desk. That is, until I remembered I was wearing a skirt. I mean, there was no easy way to pull off that maneuver gracefully.

"Mom, I have to go. My boss just walked in. I'll call you later." I held up a finger to let Barry know I'd be right with him. He shifted impatiently and mouthed the words, "I have to get to a meeting."

Mom shouted into the receiver, "You're always putting your job before your family! Find yourself a nice Italian man to marry, and have babies. Then you won't have to worry about being interrupted by a boss." I could hear the hurt and anger in her voice. "You go ahead and take care of some stranger's needs before your mother," she said, and she slammed the receiver in my ear.

I pretended she was still on the other end of the phone. I didn't want my new boss to know that my mother had just hung up on me.

"Okay, I'll check in later today. Bye." I pushed the button to end the call and asked, "Do you need something?"

"Yeah, I forgot to mention that we have a staff meeting this afternoon at three in the conference room down the hall."

"A staff meeting?"

He smiled at my inquisitiveness. "I've been out of the office. It's a good way for me to get caught up, don't you think? Victoria is putting together the minutes from the last few meetings for you to see what's been going on. We always use the same conference room, but for the life of me I can't remember the number. Anyway, ask her to tell you where it is. See you later."

"Sure. I'll head over to see her right now." I looked down at his cane. "How's the knee feeling?"

"A little better. Using the cane takes the pressure off. It should be fine by tomorrow."

"Boy, that's a relief. I really don't want to be known as the knee-basher."

He smiled but didn't answer, then turned to leave. I followed him as he limped down the hall . . . enjoying the view immensely.

I approached Victoria's desk as she stapled the last set of minutes.

"These are for you. It didn't take him long to get you into the middle of things, did it?"

"Oh, I'm thrilled he's giving me something to do. Too much pampering is not a good thing."

"I can assure you, Barry doesn't pamper. If anything, he's a bit of a slave driver." She hesitated for a moment, and the look on her face told me she regretted her words.

Jokingly I said, "I knew it! You two have been pulling the wool over my eyes so I'd think you were nice."

Victoria rolled her eyes. "You got me. The 'nice' act is only for today." She smiled. "Tomorrow we bring on the big guns."

"That's what I was afraid of." I turned to leave.

"How about lunch?"

"Lunch?" I said reluctantly, checking my watch. "It'll have to be a short one, so I can go over all the material you're giving me before the meeting."

"That's fine. We don't have to go very far. We can eat at the diner in the lobby." She handed me the stack of minutes. "Take these back to your office, grab your wallet, and meet me here."

"Okay. I'll be right back."

We took the elevator down to the lobby level and walked into the restaurant, a burger-and-fries place. A crowd of customers stood waiting to place their take-out orders. The hostess ushered us to a corner booth.

"So, what do you think?" Victoria said, sliding into one of the slick blue seats. "Feeling a little overwhelmed yet?"

I laughed. "I'll be fine."

"Of course you will. No one expects you to be perfect your first day. Maybe tomorrow, though," she teased. "Isn't he gorgeous?"

"Who?" I turned my head to look around the room.

"Barry . . . isn't he hot?"

"He's a nice-looking man," I answered nonchalantly. "And I'll bet his wife is just as gorgeous." *How's that for being coy?*

She shook her head. "No, no, no," she said, "he's not married. He says he's a confirmed bachelor, but I know he's afraid to get involved again. He was supposed to be married, but his fiancée got cold feet at the last minute and bailed on him."

"I'm sorry to hear that, although I understand completely."

Victoria's eyes widened with surprise. "Why? Did someone do that to you too?"

"No, I recently broke off my own engagement. Not because I developed cold feet. We just had completely different goals."

Hmm, so the fox is a bachelor.

There was no doubt in my mind that I was in for some tough sledding, rubbing shoulders with this man.

We finished eating, and I headed back to my office to read the minutes from the previous staff meetings. I studied the documents until Victoria buzzed me on the intercom to announce the time. I scurried around my office, trying to locate my portfolio so I could take notes, then headed in the direction of the conference room.

Mentally on overload, I opened the door and was surprised to see so many people in attendance. I'd thought I met most of them that morning, but evidently they were only the tip of this iceberg. The long conference table in the center of the room was covered with trays of fruits, cookies, and cakes. I looked around and didn't immediately recognize anyone except Ryan Garrett, who winked and smiled when he saw me. People began approaching me to introduce themselves. As soon as Barry spotted me, he walked toward me—without the use of a cane.

"Welcome." He dragged me into a clearing and held up his free hand.

"Ladies and gentlemen, may I have your attention?" The room became silent. "I'd like you to meet Cassie Pirelli, the newest member of our staff. Cassie will be working directly for me as my executive assistant. She'll help prepare my presentations, she'll be the lead conference coordinator, and at times she'll travel to marketing conferences with me. Please give her a warm welcome."

I'd be traveling with him—Foxy Guy? Gulp.

After he concluded, everyone applauded, and those I hadn't met walked up to welcome me.

"Are there always so many people at staff meetings?" I asked Barry in between handshakes.

"No. This isn't a usual meeting."

"It's not?"

"It seems the secretarial staff had their own ideas in mind for today. They wanted to meet you and welcome me back." He gestured toward a group standing in one corner of the room. "Those people are the department heads," he said. "Usually you and I meet with them. But that'll have to wait until tomorrow." He grinned. "In the interest of morale, though, we do try to have gatherings like this now and then. It's a good way for the employees to bond."

"All righty, then. I think I'll go do some bonding myself."

As I made my way around the room, I noticed another cute guy watching me rather intently. He was tall, dark, and handsome and gave new meaning to the word *sexy*. With chocolate brown hair and hazel eyes, he managed to attract the attention of every female in that conference room.

Our eyes made a connection, and he walked over to meet me. My heart thought it was an Olympic skater and performed a triple axel.

"Hi, Cassie. I'm Jason Reed."

I smiled. "Hello, Jason. Pleased to meet you."

He gave me a full, sexy smile. "I can assure you, the pleasure is all mine."

Chapter Three

With the first week on the job under my belt, I shopped most of Saturday, then decided to treat myself to a manicure and pedicure. I was going to enjoy the fruits of my laborious workweek. Megan, with whom I shared an apartment in Nutley, was off spending the day with her mother, and we never caught up until Sunday morning.

That Sunday morning I entered her bedroom, placed the cup of coffee I'd brought in for her on the nightstand, and paced back and forth, eager for her to wake up. I thought she'd stir with the amount of noise I was making, but she was out like a light.

"Hey, Megan," I said loudly. "Wake up. Coffee's ready." I picked the cup back up and held it under her nose, trying to lure her out of her deep slumber. I'd already been up for hours due to an acute case of anxiety over telling my parents about my new life.

"Oh, go away," she said as she rolled over onto her side, pulling the covers up over her head. I pinched her big toe through the coverlet, and she sat up, her long hair in disarray, covering most of her face. She squinted through half-closed eyes at the clock on her dresser. "What are you doing up so early?" she said, placing her hand above her eyes to shield her from the bright sunlight. She groaned and flopped back down into a prone position.

"Megan, c'mon. I'm nervous, and I need to talk to you."

"About what?" she mumbled.

"Today is Sunday. Pirelli Family Fest. Any of this ringing a bell with you?"

"Yeah, the same thing we do every Sunday," she said, slurring her words.

"Meg!" I shouted. "Have you forgotten what we're going to tell my parents today?"

She jolted upright. "Oh, yeah, right. I guess I did." She rubbed her eyes and tried to focus on my face. When she began to zero in on what I'd just said, she raised her eyebrows in surprise.

"Wait a minute, girlfriend. You said *we're* going to tell them. You mean"—she pointed a manicured finger at me—"*you're* going to tell them. But, hey, that's no big deal, right?"

"How can you say that?" I bellowed. "I've been lying

to my mother all week, and now I'm going to announce one more thing she can hold against me for the rest of my life."

She accepted the coffee and took a few sips. "Okay, give me a minute to collect my thoughts." She downed another gulp. "Okay, I'm ready. Let me hear what you're going to say. Take it from the top."

"Thanks, Meg. I knew you wouldn't mind if I woke you up early. Actually, I tried not to, but practicing in front of the mirror wasn't cutting it." I sighed. "All right, let me go through this one more time." I took a deep breath and rubbed my eyes. Thoughts began crowding my mind, and I decided I needed reassurance first, before I practiced my speech.

"I know this anxiety is absolutely ridiculous, but Mom's such a control freak, she totally intimidates me."

Megan's face was posed in a smirk while she waited patiently for my speech to begin.

I spilled my guts instead. "I know I'll be fine, but I need to be prepared to ward off the evil comments she'll be shoveling out today." Megan placated me with a nod. "She's not over my broken engagement yet, and you know what that means. Can't you just hear her now?"

"Yeah, I can hear her. But the fact of the matter is that you've been through this drill before. I really don't understand why you're so nervous. It's not as if you're underage—you're an adult living on your own, for Pete's sake. You don't need her approval—so stop asking for it. You need to be strong and tell her what you're doing. If you present a positive attitude, she'll go with the flow. If you act wishy-washy, you'll give her the upper hand, and she'll continue to act out her aggression."

"You're absolutely right."

"Okay, Cass, take a deep breath and relax. I'll pretend to be your mother." She arched her eyebrows, trying to imitate one of Mom's facial expressions.

I laughed. "Oh, man, you really do look like her."

"Good." She handed me one of the pillows from her bed. "Here, take this. You need to relieve some of that tension first."

With her pillow in position, she commanded, "Put up your dukes." And in an instant she began hitting me over the head. It reminded me of our teenage pajama parties.

I returned the favor, smacking my pillow on her head.

"Go ahead. I dare you to hit me back harder."

I became more aggressive and slammed down the pillow over and over. I was having fun but, more important, beginning to feel better. We pounded each other fast and furiously until we were blinded by the feathers that spurted out of her pillows. Then we both fell backward onto the bed, exhausted and laughing.

Megan's long hair had flown all over the place in our pillow fight. Several strands were stuck in her mouth from laughing. She brushed them away, still laughing. When she regained her composure, she sat upright.

"Phew," she said. "Do you feel better now?"

"I do. That was fun, and I'm not feeling as frustrated.

So I guess I need to buy a punching bag to use whenever I'm anxious . . . and to replace your pillow."

"That's a good idea. Are you ready to let me hear your speech? I'll play devil's advocate—or your mother," she teased.

I picked up a pillow and threw it at her. "I really appreciate the way you keep me grounded. You have an uncanny knack for putting things into perspective by making me see how silly I'm being."

After we finished getting ready, we left the apartment and walked to the car.

"What are you grinning about over there, Ms. Cassie?" Megan asked as we drove out of the parking lot, ready to face the music at my parents' house.

"I was just thinking about how wonderful it feels to be liberated, doing my own thing, even though I'm about to face the self-appointed Queen of Guilt." I sighed and lost the smile. "I know she's going to be hurling criticisms at me today. I wish, just once, the woman would say she's proud of me . . . that I can do anything I put my mind to."

"Well, she may not say it to you, or in front of you, but she's proud of you. She just has a difficult time expressing it, that's all."

"Yeah, right," I snickered. "She sure as heck doesn't have a difficult time expressing the negative comments."

"Yeah, but that's who she is. She has control issues. Besides, having an only child is tough on parents. They want you to have everything. Of course, there's a price to pay. You're supposed to want what they want for you." She scrunched up her face. "As far as Tony is concerned, though, you did the right thing by breaking off the engagement."

"Oh, wait," I said. "I haven't told you the latest. Francine Mancuso called me the other day with some interesting tidbits about the Sisters of Italy." I chuckled.

"The Sisters of Italy?" We both laughed. "You're a nut. Okay, I'll bite. What is your mother up to now?"

"Francine said I added insult to injury when I broke off my engagement with Tony."

"Boy, your list of demerits gets longer all the time," Megan said.

"Yeah, I'll say, but then, that's nothing new. Anyway, brace yourself for this one. Francine told me that Mom and her friends have an ongoing bet as to whose daughter will get married first."

Megan's big blue eyes opened wide in surprise, and she released a gasp. "No way. You're kidding, right?" She laughed hysterically. "But, knowing your mother, anything's possible. She's such a hoot."

"Yeah," I said sarcastically. "She's a real hoot, all right." I looked at her. "You know what's next, don't you?"

Megan nodded. "Yep. She's not going to let up until she gets you to agree to a date with Sammy Scarliotti. Right?"

"Right, but now I understand why she's in such a

hurry. She was the front-runner until I broke my engagement, but now Josephine Cici's in first place."

"Are you kidding me?" She giggled and smacked her thigh. "Your mother's archrival?"

"That's the one. No wonder she's working so hard at setting the stage for me to join forces with the slinging-pasta-and-having-babies sorority. I wish I could make her understand that I don't want any part of that. At least not now. Do you remember her telling me I'd never make it in the corporate world?"

"I do, but I don't think she meant to hurt your feelings. She was just trying to convince you that marriage and babies are the proper goals of every young woman." She shook her head. "You should write a book about your family. No one would ever believe it."

"That's for sure. The other thing I learned from Francine is why Sammy's so appealing to Mom. The Scarliotti family has a slew of kids running around. So if Sammy's such a hot prospect, why does he need his aunt to fix him up? What's the matter, can't he find his own girlfriends?"

I groaned when we pulled into the parking lot behind my parents' building.

"It's okay, kiddo," Megan encouraged, patting me on the shoulder. "You're going to do fine. Just present a positive attitude, and ignore your mother's guilt tactics."

Chapter Four

Sundays are special in the Pirelli household. That's when the entire clan gathers around our large dining room table for a feast. Spending time with the family is always a treat, but Mom's cooking is the highlight of the day for me. She and Dad run a small catering service out of his Italian deli.

The rich smell of tomatoes, garlic, and basil permeated the entire fourth-floor hallway, leading the way to their apartment.

When I opened the door to enter, Megan and I were nearly blinded by the thick fog created by the Italian stogies the males of the family smoked as they sat around shooting the bull and drinking Uncle Nicky's homemade wine.

We made our way to the kitchen unnoticed. The

aunts, who were lined up in a row, ready to head to the dining room, all nodded their greetings. One by one they filed past us like a bucket brigade carrying huge serving platters with steaming hot food. I was happy to see all my favorites, like pasta puttanesca, chicken cacciatore, vitello parmigiano y melanzana, and the best, a huge basket of homemade garlic bread for sopping up every last drop of sauce. This was comfort food at its finest.

Mom looked up and said, "Hey, you two are just in time." She handed me a large wooden bowl overflowing with lettuce. "Cassie, you carry the salad, and, Megan, grab the extra sauce bowl from the counter next to the stove, will you?"

There's never a shortage of food in this family. I leaned over and kissed my mother on the cheek. "Hi, Mom. Mmm, it smells yummy in here."

"That must mean you're hungry."

"I'll say," I assured her. "That's an understatement. We passed on breakfast this morning for fear we'd spoil our appetites."

I waited until everyone filled their plates with food before delivering my good news. I pushed my chair back, stood, and tapped my fork on a glass.

"Hey, everybody, may I have your attention? I have something wonderful I want to share with all of you."

Good, positive sales pitch, Cass.

I looked at Megan, who was smiling at me, and tried to do what she'd suggested. *Present a confident attitude.*

"You're getting married!" my mother shouted, clutching her chest.

I sighed and did some internal eye-rolling. "Mom, you have a one-track mind. No, I'm not getting married."

"Well, what other news could be better than that?"

"Mother. Stop already!"

I glanced around the table at my family. The room fell silent, and everyone looked up and stared at me as if I were an alien.

"I've just started a new job—the opportunity of a lifetime," I announced with pride in my voice. "Ta-da. I'm working for the New York based Merrill Finance Company."

"What do you mean you have a new job?" Mom asked. "Doing what?"

"I'm the executive assistant to the vice president of marketing. I'm lead coordinator for conferences, and I'll be dealing with customers, helping to prepare sales presentations, and a gazillion other things I don't know about yet. It's always fun learning new things, don't you think?"

She stared at me, her big brown eyes open wide.

I shrugged. "It was an offer I couldn't refuse, so I took it."

"But what about your job with that big shot attorney . . . Mr. what's his name?" Her voice screeched like a cop's whistle. "Besides, you shouldn't be working at all. You should be concentrating on finding a husband."

Mom is a short, overweight woman who enjoys

eating as much as she does cooking. Shouting is typical in the Pirelli household, especially when Mom thinks she's losing control over her family. She has a set of lungs that could rock the Empire State Building. My stomach tightened in knots as my eyes surveyed the table.

The relatives were hunched over their plates, silently shoveling food into their mouths like robots. They do this when Mom's on one of her tirades. She has the entire family trained well, and most know when to keep their mouths shut. That is, all except Aunt Mary, who doesn't know when to lock her lips and throw away the key.

She's Mom's older sister and always has something to say. I guess it runs in the family. Her eyes narrowed in a glare as she opened her mouth to speak.

Oh, boy, here it comes.

"Your mother is right, Cassie. Why do you want another job? A nice girl like you should be 'working' to find another man to marry, not on your career."

Needless to say, Aunt Mary is not one of my favorite relatives, but it would be disrespectful for me to ask her to refrain from voicing her opinion. Every week she sits in the same chair, arms crossed, her right eyebrow arched, and waits for a bomb to drop so she can add more fuel to the fire.

The eldest sister among five children, Aunt Mary was born and raised in the little town of Calabria, Italy. The family migrated to the States before Mom was born. Although Mom is considered a New World Italian by Aunt Mary's standards, Mary never gives up when it comes to trying to instill her sense of values and family traditions in everyone.

I shot her a dirty look and directed my attention toward my mother. "Mom, an opportunity like this comes along once in a lifetime."

I looked around the table again, hoping one of the relatives would speak up on my behalf. *Yeah, right.* I glanced at Megan, who was pulling on her earlobe— the agreed-upon gesture we chose earlier as a sign of encouragement, which meant, *You go, girl.*

Out of the corner of my eye I could see Mom moving an arm back and forth.

Oh, boy, she's doing the violin thing again.

Mom's known for her melodrama. We're all used to the ritual, so I just ignored her and continued. "So, my heart tells me this is a good move for my future."

"Oh, yeah, and *my* heart tells me you should be getting married and having babies," Mom said. "Having this job will take you away from your family."

Without skipping a beat, she continued. "You know, Maria's nephew, Sammy, really wants to meet you. He comes from a good Italian family and has a successful business on Wall Street."

Here it comes. I cut her off before she could start up again. "Oh, Mother, puh-leeze, he's not my type."

"How do you know? You don't even know him."

"Well, I've done some checking around, and he doesn't sound like the kind of guy I'm interested in."

She looked at me, a big grin on her face. "So you checked him out, huh? I guess there's hope for you after all."

Man, I was kicking myself for admitting that one. The woman just gets me so frustrated, I find myself saying things to appease her. Only this time it backfired.

"No. I was giving him the benefit of the doubt for your sake, so I thought I'd check with some people to see if they knew him. The things I heard told me we have nothing in common."

Mom sat with a smug look on her face as though she knew otherwise. Man, I hate when she does that.

I continued. "You like him because there are lots of babies running around in the Scarliotti family, and every female is always pregnant!"

Aunt Mary's eyes glazed over. She shouted in support of Mom, "Cassie, your mother only wants what's best for you!"

If only Aunt Mary could take my side once in a while, it would make a big difference. But that's not likely to happen. The two sisters get themselves so worked up, their voices begin to collide, trying to be heard above the other. Did I tell you this was another Italian trait?

I glanced over at Dad, who seemed to be handling my announcement well. But poor Dad didn't stand a chance against these two. He's one of those quiet men who learned early in his marriage to choose his battles wisely. He's a short, thin man who had thick, dark ringlets covering the top of his head in his heyday, but all that remains now is a shiny dome, if you know what I mean. The hair around the circumference of his head looks like a clown's wig.

"What's wrong with that?" Mom asked defiantly, continuing her support for the Scarliotti baby factory.

"What's wrong with that is simple. I'm a career woman now, and I'm not ready to settle down. I know you'll find this hard to believe, but there's more to life than slinging pasta and having babies. My goal is to climb to the top of the corporate ladder."

"Good, so climb!" she said in a huffy tone. "You wouldn't have to reach for any goal if you became involved with Sammy. He has a lot to offer. You could have anything you wanted with the kind of money he makes."

"Ma, do you have any idea what kind of business Sammy has?"

"No, but Maria tells me he always has a wad of money—and, after all, it is on Wall Street."

"Ma, he owns a hot dog wagon. He slings dogs for a living!"

She made the sign of the cross, then placed her two hands together as though she was about to pray. "What are you talking about? He's a nice boy, and so what if it's a hot dog wagon? It's an honest living."

"Okay, Mom, maybe he is a nice boy. He just doesn't sound like the right one for me, and I'm not going through that again." I sat down and began to eat in silence. I'd known she was going to rain on my parade. Why should today be any different than any other day? Still, frustration gnawed at my stomach. Why did I always look for her approval? When was I going to learn that that was just wishful thinking on my part? The only news that was going to make this woman happy was an announcement of my betrothal and my preparation to become a mass producer in my very own baby factory.

NaNu, my grandfather, gave me a compassionate look and flashed his wide, toothy smile, exposing the glitter of his two gold front teeth. I smiled back at him and threw him a kiss. I'm NaNu's favorite relation. He's never told me that, but I can tell. For as long as I can remember, upon greeting me he holds my face in his hands and smothers it with kisses. Then the cheek-pinching routine begins as he says in his native language, "*Mia bella piccola, mia perfetta ragazza.*"

I have no idea what he's saying, except I think *bella* means *beautiful*. The only time my parents spoke the language was when I was growing up and they didn't want me to know what they were discussing.

Mom released a sudden theatrical gasp, loud enough to startle the next-door neighbors, not to mention everyone around our table.

"Cassie, did you say this Merrill Finance Company is based in New York? As in, New York City?"

"Yes, that's the one," I said, smiling with nervous anticipation, waiting for the bomb to drop.

"Are you out of your mind?" Her hands began flying

all over the place. "You took a job away from the family without discussing it with us first?" She posed her face in a puppy dog pout. "The next thing you'll be telling us is that you're moving to the city too."

I sat erect—slouching is a dead giveaway that Mom is winning the argument. Megan kept tugging on her ear. Mom stopped talking and looked at Megan. "Do you have an earache, honey?"

"Oh. No," she said, shaking her head. "I just had my ears pierced the other day, and it's a little itchy."

I tried to squelch a laugh. *Is that Megan fast on her feet, or what?*

I glanced at Mom, who remained in the throes of pouting, the tip-off that the silent treatment is mere seconds away. I decided to beat her at her own game and continued to enjoy my food. Other than the sound of forks clicking as they hit the plates, it was so quiet in that room, you could hear a pin drop.

At last, halfway through the meal, I could see Mom fidgeting in her seat, and I knew she couldn't stand it any longer.

"So? You never answered my question. Are you moving to New York City?"

I cleared my throat and looked at Megan. "Actually, Megan and I will be looking for something in Greenwich Village."

There, its right out in the open.

Megan grinned and gave me a discreet thumbs-up.

I continued, "You know how long Megan's been

making the trip into the city. She's always complaining about the commute." I gave my friend the wide-eyed stare, wanting her to take over, but she didn't take the hint, so I led her into it. "Tell her, Meg."

"Yeah, driving into the city every day is a long haul. It should only take an hour, but instead it's taking almost two. I've even considered taking the train, but that's so expensive."

Mom nodded in disgust, then turned to look at me. "So there's your answer. Why work in the city when you can walk to work here?"

"The pay scale is much higher in New York than in New Jersey," Megan said, unconsciously doing the ear-tug again.

Mom interrupted her. "Boy, that ear is really bothering you, isn't it? Maybe we should call Dr. Lorenzo. He's probably home from church by now."

"No. That's okay, Mama P. I have antibiotic cream with me." She grinned.

I stifled a giggle.

"So this whole job thing is about money?" Mom said, looking at me. She pursed her lips in anger. "And this is supposed to make me feel better?" She shook her head in disgust. "You're moving away from your family because you can make more money?"

"Well, you seem to think it was important that Sammy makes a lot of money."

"That's different. The man's supposed to be the provider."

I gulped hard. I didn't know what else to say to that comment. "*This* is about opportunity. This is about growing as a person."

"Oh, I get it. You can't grow here in Nutley?"

I raised a hand like a stop sign. "Okay, I'm finished."

Megan interceded. "Hey, Mama P., you know I'll keep an eye on her."

"That's what scares me. Who's going to keep an eye on you? The two of you together are like the blind leading the blind." She turned her attention back to me and asked, "How long have you been working at this job?"

Just as I was about to open my mouth, her eyes glowed like a lightbulb, and she interrupted. "Oh, wait a minute. *That's* why you couldn't have lunch with us last week, isn't it?" She gave me the tilted head and arched eyebrows look.

"Yes, and I'm sorry I didn't tell you right away," I lied. "But honestly, I wanted to make sure I was going to like the job first before I got you all upset about my not working here in Nutley." Talk about being fast on your feet. I was catching on to Megan's routine.

Dad finally opened his mouth. "Lucy, stop making Cassie feel like this is an inquisition. She's twenty-five years old. She's a woman, not a child."

"Michael, I'm afraid she'll get mugged by some lunatic." She released a groan, rested her elbows on the table, and propped her chin on her fingertips. "When she moves there, you can kiss peaceful sleep good-bye." To intensify the drama she said, "Cassie, I can't believe you're doing this to me."

With this kind of performance, the woman's headed right for an Academy Award nomination in the Best Actress category.

"I can take care of myself," I said with confidence.

"Yeah, right! All five feet, two inches of you."

Aunt Mary smacked her forehead with one hand and shouted, "*Mama mia!*" She made the sign of the cross and kissed her thumb. I've never quite figured out why that's part of the ritual—you know, the kissing of the thumb thing. I forced myself to focus my attention on the immediate discussion.

"Listen, the new boss may think I'm so wonderful, he'll give me my own limo driver."

Now, *that* got their attention, and everyone, except Mom, stood and began doing the tarantella, the traditional wedding dance. They frequently practiced the tarantella as a reminder to me that I was next in line to get married. After I broke off my engagement to Tony, they stopped doing the dance for a while. Mom said it was too painful to watch.

Needless to say, she's trying to win the Sisters of Italy bet, and it's driving her crazy that she's not having much luck convincing me.

Raising her hands in defeat, she said, "Okay, Cassie, I give up. I know my opinion doesn't count. You're going to do what you want anyway." She cleared her throat. "And for the record, young lady, I will worry

about my only daughter until I can no longer breathe."
She sighed. "So tell me. Just how soon do I start losing
sleep at night from worry?"

Brace yourself for the grand finale.

"It's a good thing I slept well last night," Mom said
nasally. "If only I'd known this was happening, I could
have started taking a few catnaps during the day to
keep up my strength." The pout returned. "When do
you and Megan move into the new place?"

I rolled my eyes and shook my head in disbelief. Is
this woman a pro, or what? It's a wonder she's not on
Broadway.

"We're still looking."

Mom got a glint in her eyes. "Oh, good. That gives me
more time to rest up before you make the big move. I'll
never get another night's rest once you live in the city."

Dad intervened. "Lucy, give it a rest, will you? When
was the last time you slept through the night? Before
menopause?"

"Oh, shut up, Michael!" she yelled indignantly.
"This is our daughter we're talking about here." She
turned to face me. "I hope you're not planning to live
there when you finally stop this foolishness and get
married and have kids. If you do, I just know I'll never
get to know my grandchildren."

I didn't respond. I mean, really, what was the point?

The meal finished, the women got up to clear the
table, and the men returned to the living room to light
their stogies and drink more wine.

Megan pulled me over to a corner of the room, hugged me, and whispered in my ear, "You did a great job, Cass. Stay strong. Trust me, this is going to be the best decision you've ever made."

I returned her hug as tears welled in my eyes. "Thanks, Meg. I appreciate your support."

She picked up her handbag and walked over to Mom. "I have to leave now. I'm going over to see my mom. Thank you for a wonderful meal. You're still the best cook in Nutley, Mama P."

Mom gave her a broad smile and headed back to the dining room. "You sure you don't want me to call Dr. Lorenzo about that ear?"

She smiled. "No thanks. I applied some cream to my earlobe. It's actually feeling better."

Shortly after, Megan left and I headed to the kitchen to help with the cleanup. An hour later, when all the dishes were done, I reached for a towel to dry my hands.

"Phew," I said. "We sure do use a lot of dishes, don't we?"

Mom nodded. I guess she was still in a bad mood after learning my plans.

I left the kitchen and began gathering my things to leave. No point in hanging around—I wasn't in any mood for the debate to kick up again.

All the aunts and uncles were still sitting around. The men were getting louder by the minute—the result of too much wine. Aunt Mary sat with her sisters, giving them all advice about how to raise their children. Aunt

Mary is an aging spinster who didn't have children. How she became an authority is beyond me.

NaNu was fast asleep in his rocker, head tilted back, mouth wide open, snoring as loudly as a buzz saw cutting through a log.

I turned when I heard Mom call out my name. She was carrying a tray of biscotti in one hand, a pot of coffee in the other.

"Cassie, give me a hand here, will you?"

"Sure." I reached for the coffeepot as she passed around the tray.

"Are you leaving already?" she asked. "Aw, can't you stay a little longer? Come." She nodded in the direction of a chair. "Sit down. Have some coffee."

"Mom, I can't. I need to get back to the apartment. I have an early day tomorrow."

"Oh, that's right." She tipped her head to one side, an annoyed look on her face. "I forgot. The new job."

I let the comment slide.

Aunt Mary groaned when she saw the cookies. "Lucy, have mercy. I've already eaten too much. I think I'll smoke a stogie instead." She shouted, "Hey, Nicky, let me have one of your cigars!"

He looked at her as though she had two heads. "Are you crazy? You won't like the taste of these stogies."

She arched an eyebrow. "Whaddaya mean? You men smoke them to help you digest your food. Why can't I?" I guess that was her feeble attempt at convincing us she was a New World Italian instead of an Old World Italian.

"Okay, if you really want one." He put a fresh one into his mouth. "I'll even light it for you."

I leaned over to kiss Mom, snickering at Aunt Mary's outrageous behavior.

"Oh, wait," Mom said, "I have something for you." She walked into the hall to the alcove she used as a shrine. St. Anthony was proudly perched atop the cabinet, his feet illuminated by the glow of votive candles. A picture of the Pope adorned the wall above it, and Mary and Joseph faced each other from opposite walls.

I watched as she pulled open a drawer and removed something from it. She turned and placed a small satin pouch in my hand. Puzzled, I opened it to check the contents and couldn't help but smile.

"What are these for?" As if I really needed to ask.

"Hey, if you insist on working in the city, then you'd better make sure you carry these beads in your purse. I'm counting on you to say this Rosary every day, as will the family. Oh, and cut your hair. I've read articles that say women with long hair are at a higher risk of being mugged because the mugger can latch on to it and drag his victim into a car. We need to keep you safe from those crazy people who prey on young women."

"Absolutely. And these beads will be right next to the Bible in my handbag." I grinned. "Thank you for your thoughtfulness, but, Mom, I'll be working uptown. It's very safe there."

"What? You don't think crime happens in those high-society areas?" She raised her eyebrows and gave me the *look*. You know, the one every parent uses to tell their offspring to button their lips.

Ready to walk out the door, Aunt Josie handed me another parcel. She looked at Mom. "You forgot to give Cassie her care package, Lucy."

"Thank you, Josie. Yeah, here's some food for the week. You're so skinny, God knows what you eat. At least I won't worry about your starving if I give you something to put into that empty refrigerator of yours." She knit her brows. "You do know how to reheat this stuff, don't—"

I interrupted, "Yes, Mother, I do know how to reheat food. Thank you very much." I turned to leave, then chuckled when the rest of the family lined up on both sides of the hall to bid me farewell and wish me luck.

This is my colorful family. They're boisterous, demanding, and a little crazy, but I still love them.

After all the well-wishing, I was finally able to make my escape, closing the door behind me. I walked down the hallway and heard my father's voice in a faint whisper.

"Pssst, Cassie!"

I turned my head in the direction of his voice, but it was so dark, I couldn't see him. The overhead light in the corner where he stood was out. I spotted the lit end of his cigar as he took a drag.

I whispered back, "Dad, take another puff so I can find you."

He inhaled so many times in succession, he started coughing like an old car grinding to start.

I located him and slapped his back to help him. "Dad, are you all right?"

"Shh. I don't want your mother to hear us," he said between coughs. "I'm fine."

"Why are you hiding in a corner of the hallway?"

"Your mother is worried about your going into the city, and I didn't want her to know I was worried too, because then she'll worry about my being worried."

"Dad-dy," I said as though I was twelve again, "please don't worry. I'm going to be just fine. Honest."

"Yes, you are, because you're going to take this with you."

"What? What am I taking with me?"

He grabbed hold of the medal hanging around his neck.

I did an internal eye-roll, thinking I was soon going to need a U-Haul to carry all their gifts.

"I want you to wear my St. Christopher's medal. St. Chris has watched over me all these years, and now I want you to have it."

My father's compassion melted my heart, and I smiled in admiration. "I love you, Dad."

He removed the medallion from around his neck and hooked it onto mine. He stepped back and gazed at it with a look of pride on his face. "I'm very proud of you Cassie. I know you'll be careful."

"Thanks for the vote of confidence, Dad. Now go inside before I start bawling and Mom hears us."

Relieved I'd purged my angst by delivering word of my new job to my mother, I walked into my apartment feeling as though I'd just walked out of the confessional at St. Mary's. All those years Mom spent spoon-feeding me guilt were paying off—for her, that is. Not that I was going to change my mind about the job, but she'd be proud of her accomplishment had she known I'd been feeling guilty all week.

I entered my kitchen and placed the food in the refrigerator, eager to get a good night's sleep. I dropped down onto my bed, ready to crawl under the covers, when the phone rang. I checked the clock and immediately tensed, wondering what bad news was coming my way at 11:30 at night. I hate late-night calls—they always scare me—so I quickly grabbed the receiver.

"Hello?"

"Sorry to call you so late, Cassie."

"What's wrong, Mom?" I asked in a panic. "Is everyone okay?"

"Oh, it's nothing, dear."

"So you called me . . . why?"

"Well, I just finished talking to Maria. You know my friend Maria, don't you?"

Here it comes.

"Yes, I know your friend Maria," I said in a grudging voice. "What about her?"

"Well, I need a really big favor from you."

"What?" I asked sharply, knowing where this was headed.

"Would you please just go on one date with Sammy?"

"No. No. No," I said emphatically. "I don't want to."

"You never know, he might turn out to be Mr. Right."

"Mom, I'm not looking for Mr. Right. Furthermore, I don't need anyone to fix me up on a date. I do quite well on my own."

"Please, do this for me. I don't want to hurt Maria's feelings."

"Oh, stop! This isn't about Maria. It's about you making a last-ditch effort to get me to stay in New Jersey. It's also about losing that bet to Mrs. Cici, isn't it?"

"Of course not! I just want you to meet him, that's all."

"Well, you can forget it. I'm not doing it."

"And how do *you* know there's a bet?"

"Aha! So it *is* true."

"Listen, Cassie," she said, raising her voice a few decibels. "That's the least you can do after lying to me all week. You owe me. You broke my heart when you dumped Tony. He was a nice young man who had a lot to offer, and you threw it all away for a career. You broke his heart too, and now I can't even look his mother in the eye when I see her in the market."

So the truth finally cometh. I checked the clock and knew the woman was never going to give up until I agreed. I was tired, annoyed, and just wanted to get some sleep. I acquiesced, deciding it was the only way I was ever going to get her off my back.

"Okay," I sighed, "but *only* if you agree to invite him for dinner with the rest of the family around."

Excited, she said, "Oh, thanks, Cassie—I knew you wouldn't let me down."

I'd just sold my soul to the devil, but I needed to put an end to this Sammy thing once and for all.

"Now I'll be able to hold my head up in this neighborhood. I'm going to call Maria right now to tell her. She'll be so excited, and I know Sammy will be too. He's heard so much about you from Maria, he's been eager to date you for a long time. So when can you make it?"

"Gee, Mom, don't rush on my account."

"Well, I'd like to make it as soon as possible."

"I'm afraid I can't make it too soon. I'm involved in a very time-consuming project at the office. I don't think I can set a date right now."

"Can't you at least give me something?"

"All right, let's say the week after next."

"Can't you be more specific? You know, you're making a commitment here. And don't you dare pretend you can't make it by coming up with some lame excuse at the last minute. I mean, after all, everyone will be accommodating your schedule."

"Yeah, yeah, I know." I released a deep sigh. "Wait a minute, and let me get my calendar out of my purse." I put the phone down on my bed and grabbed my purse off the dresser. With calendar in hand, I walked back and picked up the phone. I leafed through the pages, checking for an opening. "Okay, how about a week from next Friday?"

"Okay. Thank you, Cass. Someday, when I'm gone, you'll look back on this moment with great pride, knowing you fulfilled a wish for your mother."

"Yeah, fine, whatever. I'm going to bed now." I placed the phone back in its cradle and made my way back to my bed. Exhausted, I dropped onto the mattress and pulled the covers snugly under my chin. My anxiety returned when I recounted the conversation, and I knew this was going to be one of those times when I would hate myself in the morning.

Chapter Five

Before I knew it two weeks had passed, and the dreaded date with Sammy Scarliotti was the next day. I left the office and returned home, eager to talk to Megan. Maybe she could come up with some plausible excuse.

I entered the apartment. Megan was on the phone. She smiled at me as I passed on the way to my bedroom to get out of my office clothes. When I returned, she was reading a magazine.

"How was your day?" she asked.

"It was okay. How was yours?"

"Well, from the look on your face, I'd say my day was better than yours. What's going on?"

"Um, I have a date with Sammy tomorrow night," I confessed.

"You what?" She began to laugh hysterically. "When did this come up?"

I explained how it had happened.

"And you're telling me this after two weeks? Why didn't you say something sooner?"

"Quite frankly, I was embarrassed that I'd allowed my mother to convince me. So do you think you can help me come up with an excuse as to why I can't make it?"

"Not a chance. Canceling out the night before is going to cost you plenty. Your mother will never let you live it down." She shook her head. "I still can't believe you waited this long to tell me."

"I know. I'm sorry. I just couldn't bring myself to admit it. I guess I figured if I didn't think about it, maybe it would go away. That's dumb, isn't it?"

"It certainly is, but now you're committed, and you have to do it." She patted my shoulder, "Hey, maybe it won't be so bad."

"Yeah, it should be about as much fun as a root canal."

Megan stood and walked to the kitchen and opened the fridge. "Oh, my," she said in a theatrical voice, "there's no food."

"And this is a big surprise to you?"

"No. I was just trying to get you to lighten up. You're all gloom and doom over there."

"Okay, I guess this is where I say, 'Let's go out to eat', or something similar."

Megan made a mocking face at me. "Stop already, will you? It's one night out of your life, for God's sake—not the end of the world."

"I know. You're right." I walked into the kitchen and opened a cupboard, looking for something chocolate. That would make me feel better. I found an empty bag of M&M's. "Oh, no!" I shouted. "They're all gone!"

"I can't imagine why," Megan said. "You've been snacking on them like crazy. Hmm," she said, frowning, "I should have realized something was up. You eat chocolate like there's no tomorrow when you're upset." She walked over to the counter to her purse and dug inside. She pulled out a small chocolate bar and handed it to me. "Here, eat!"

I gratefully accepted her offering and had it unwrapped and in my mouth within seconds.

"Now stop sulking, and get ready to go out to eat some real food."

"Hey, chocolate's real food," I said. "For me, that is. It's like the nectar of the gods. A day without chocolate is like a day without sunshine."

"Yada, yada, yada. You tell me the same thing every time I see you eating chocolate—which is quite often lately, now that I think of it. You'd better be careful before your size four turns into a size twelve." She chuckled and pointed toward the bathroom. "Now go. I'm starving!"

I gave her a salute and headed to the bathroom. A few minutes later I *was* feeling better. That itty-bitty piece of chocolate must have raised my serotonin level—which was actually a shame, since I was planning to have something chocolate for dessert.

I returned to the living room, where Megan stood tapping her foot impatiently. I picked up my purse. "Okay, I'm ready."

Later, when we returned from the diner, Megan said, "Man, I'm exhausted. I need to get some sleep."

"I'm afraid to go to sleep," I said. "When I wake up, it will be the day I have to actually go on a date with Sammy Scarliotti."

"I thought we discussed this—at length, I might add. It's one night out of your life. Besides, your family will be right there in the room with you, so it's technically not a date. It will be more like a dinner party."

"Okay." I yawned. "I guess I am tired. Good night. Thanks for listening."

"I'll be eager to hear about the big date. Sweet dreams," she said with a smirk.

I opened my eyes, trying to wake up, my mind fuzzy from sleep. I felt pangs of anxiety attacking my stomach and remembered their cause. "I've got to be out of my *freakin'* mind!" I screeched. "Go on a date with Sammy Scarliotti?"

My early-morning regrets had me considering a phone call to Mom, pretending I'd developed some dreadful, contagious disease, like chicken pox, and I couldn't honor my commitment. Unfortunately, the hand of reality smacked me in the back of the head, and I concluded that the aftereffect of canceling would be more painful than one dinner with Sammy. I slipped out from under the covers, stepped into my furry slippers, threw my robe on over my pajamas, and headed for the kitchen to make coffee. Three feet away from the door, the smell of coffee spiraled up my nostrils.

I walked into the office. Victoria jumped up to greet me. "Good morning."

"Good morning," I mumbled while I continued to walk toward my office. I was in no mood to be around anyone who was so bubbly this early in the morning—especially today.

She called after me, "What's wrong? Are you okay?"

"Sure." I snickered. "I'm fine." And I strolled into my office, swiftly closing the door behind me. I worked straight through until five-thirty, never bothering to stop for lunch. I knew if I kept myself busy, I wouldn't have to think about the dreaded blind date that I'd been steamrolled into accepting. There was no doubt Mom considered this my penance for lying to her.

Victoria must have realized it was a Do Not Disturb day, because she left me alone.

I finished the last bit of paperwork and put the files in order for Monday. My anxiety returned in anticipation of what I was facing. And I vowed that I was never going to let Mom do this to me again.

I walked out through the lobby and hailed a cab for a

ride to Penn Station. Moving to New York was going to be my salvation, my escape, and I couldn't wait to see what my new life would bring. First, though, I had to get through this miserable date with Sammy.

As I walked to the train, regrets plagued me. "Why did I agree to do this?" I said aloud. People stared at me.

I was so angry for agreeing to meet Sammy that the smell of overheated steel and sweaty bodies didn't faze me the way it usually does. The conductor walked down the aisle, punching tickets. He made his way to my seat. "Ticket, please."

"Hey, any chance we'll be late tonight?"

He thrust his chin forward. "Listen, lady, we do the best we can." He shook his head in disgust as he turned and walked away. Based on his response, I guess he thought I was being sarcastic. Passengers glared at me.

Embarrassed, I stood and announced, "Hey, I *want* to be late tonight. Really . . . I do."

A man shouted back at me, "Well, I don't! But now that you've totally ticked this guy off, he'll probably slow the train down just out of spite."

I crouched down into my seat to avoid any further confrontations and closed my eyes, hoping to fall asleep and miss my stop.

I was awakened by the loudspeaker announcing our arrival at Nutley. I followed the crowd down the stairs to the platform and slowly walked to my car, unlocked the door, slid behind the steering wheel, and started the engine. I drove the distance to my parents' home, taking my time, allowing other drivers to cut in front of me—anything to avoid this self-inflicted date.

I reached the parking lot behind my parents' apartment building and sat for a while, thinking about a recent phone conversation I'd had. One of my co-workers from the old job knew Sammy's former girlfriend, one Rosalie Fatucci. She'd given me the girl's phone number back when I'd researched the guy, but I never called.

The only reason I'd called this time was to have a good comeback after tonight's so-called date, when Mom began her relentless pitch for the guy.

The minute I mentioned Sammy's name, Rosalie had wailed like a baby. My first thought was, *Good. I'm finally going to have something negative to say about Mom's favorite prospect.*

I'd apologized for upsetting her, ready for her to tell me tons of bad stuff about him. But that hope went down the tubes in a matter of seconds. The girl told me she was still madly in love with him. Sheesh, can't I ever get a break here? I was ready to end the conversation after that declaration, but the girl wouldn't shut up about the guy. She said Sammy was the perfect boyfriend, always took her to nice places, treated her like a queen, very respectful, gave her flowers, and family meant everything to him. Actually, those are all the things *I* look for in a man—but, hey, I'm not going there. Not this chick. No siree.

I exited the car and headed toward the apartment

building. Once inside, I could smell Mom's sauce. My stomach growled. The woman knew how to cook.

I opened the door to the apartment and inhaled the aroma of rich tomato sauce.

"Okay, Cass," I mumbled, "make the best of it. It's almost over." I was so preoccupied, I never saw Mom standing in the kitchen doorway.

"What's almost over?"

Startled, I said, "Oh, nothing." I changed the subject. "Boy, I'm starved." Megan was rubbing off on me. I was picking up the fast-on-my feet routine. "What'd you make for dinner?"

"What else but your favorites?" she said proudly. "You know, the usual. Soup, eggplant parmigiana, linguine, and a special treat for doing such a wonderful thing for your mama—my homemade garlic bread."

"Sounds wonderful! I could eat a horse."

She laughed. "You always could. But that's probably because you never have any food in that house of yours."

Let it ride, Cass.

I began to relax a little, knowing Dad and the others would be at the table. After all, what could Sammy do with all of them right there? I was actually gloating that I'd pulled a fast one by suggesting we invite him to a family dinner. I leaned forward and planted a kiss on her cheek, then forced a smile.

"What's wrong with you, Cassie?" Mom said. "You look as though you've lost your best friend."

What's wrong? As if she didn't know.

"Oh, nothing," I lied. "I'm just tired. It's been a long day." I walked into the kitchen, where Dad stood stirring the sauce on the stove. I decided to hide out with him while Mom busied herself in the other room.

Sammy showed up earlier than expected. Mom was the first to greet him. I remained in the kitchen, out of sight, when she announced his arrival. I tiptoed to the door and hid to one side so I could peek out to get a gander. He wasn't what I expected. He was actually a good-looking guy. But then, looks can be deceiving. He had a thick crop of jet black wavy hair; a curl dangled down his forehead. His short-sleeved shirt exposed muscular arms.

And then I saw the most amazing thing, and my spirits lifted. The guy had a tattoo on his upper right arm. I couldn't decipher it because I was too far away, but it didn't matter. Mom hates tattoos. I praised myself for noticing. *As soon as she feasts her eyes on his arm, he's outta here.* My insides were jumping with joy. *You're dead meat now, buster.*

Mom was acting strange, like a schoolgirl, all giddy, as she stood chatting with him.

"Cassie, come out here and meet Sammy," she said sweetly.

Who is this woman?

I walked out of the kitchen. He looked up when he heard my footsteps, grinning from ear to ear. I had to admit, he did have a nice smile, but that's all I'm admitting. Then it happened. Mom noticed his tattoo. How great is that?

Good-bye, Sammy. You're history now, baby doll.

"Aw, look at Sammy's tattoo." She rubbed her fingers over it. "Your mother must be very proud to have a son like you, Sammy," she gushed. "Look, Cassie, his tattoo is a tribute to his mother. What a nice young man."

What? This coming from the woman who thinks tattoos are disgusting? *So just because it's dedicated to his mother, it's okay? Oh, gag me. Well, isn't this just great! The smooth operator made it to the head of the class in less than five minutes.*

He wore a tailored shirt, dress slacks, and tasseled loafers. I watched Mom continue to fuss over him like a teenage girl with a crush. *Oh, man, I just know she thinks this guy is her ticket to grandchildren.*

Judging from the expensive clothing he wore, I convinced myself that Sammy was selling more than hot dogs. I mean, really, a hot dog vendor making *that* kind of money? Perhaps the wagon was a front for something else—maybe he was a runner for the mob or something. He wasn't fooling me.

Mom couldn't take her eyes off him. She flashed a toothy smile and waved a bouquet of flowers in the air for me to see. Her behavior toward him was making me ill. I'd never seen her like this before.

"Cassie, look what Sammy brought for me."

"That's nice, Ma," I answered nasally. I was hoping to get a reaction from him—didn't work.

He gave me a once-over. *Ooh. Ooh.*

Now, if that had been Barry, and he wasn't my boss, it would have been a real turn-on. On second thought, it would have been a turn-on regardless of Barry's rank.

"Sammy." She put an arm around my waist, pulling me closer. "This is my daughter, Cassie. Isn't she beautiful?"

I could feel my face flush. "Oh, Mom, please stop." *Man, this is going to be a long night.*

He gave me a full, bright smile. "You're right, Mama. She's every bit as beautiful as you described."

Mama? What's that all about?

"Mama?" I said aloud. "You two sound like old friends."

"Oh, that's right. I guess I forgot to mention it," Mom said. "I was over at Maria's one day when Sammy came by to give her a box of chocolates for her birthday. Wasn't that nice?"

I looked at her and mouthed the word *Mama*? She gave me one of those "gotcha" winks. *What a setup. It's interesting she never mentioned she'd met him before.*

He extended his hand in greeting. No way was I was going to touch him. When he finally got the message, he dropped his hand to his side and brought his left arm around from behind his back, handing me a single red rose.

Yep, the guy was a smooth operator, all right. Flowers for Mom and a single red rose for me—it was obvious this guy had been around the block a few times.

"Cassie, why don't you take Sammy into the living room and get acquainted while I fix dinner?"

Acquainted? I don't want to become acquainted *with this guy. It's bad enough I have to sit through dinner with him.* I shot Mom a look, but she ignored me and left the room.

"Cassie, it's so nice to finally meet you."

I averted my eyes and forced out a chilly "Thank you." *Too bad I can't say the same for you, Bucko. And, by the way, where is everyone? It isn't like my relatives to be late to dinner.*

When we sat down on the sofa, the little weasel wedged himself so close to me, I was lodged against one cushioned armrest. I could feel the pressure of his leg, conveniently propped against mine. He talked non-stop, his arms flying all over the place. The next thing I know, this bozo's arm is brushing against my breast. I wasn't sure if the move was intentional or not. Judging from the way he looked at me when we met, I decided it was. I shot him an angry look. He ignored it and continued to talk about his hot dog wagon franchise.

Convinced he knew what he was doing with his arm, I wasn't about to let him get away with it. I interrupted, "Listen, Bucko, I don't know what kind of broads you're—"

At that moment Mom appeared in the doorway, announcing dinner. *Dinner? Where is everybody?* Sammy, too, had the strangest look on his face, but he didn't say anything. I guess he'd gotten my message.

Still, I was glad Mom came when she did, because it meant he'd be gone that much sooner. I was certain the evening would go by quickly—especially with my parents present. We headed for the dining room.

Just let him try something with Dad sitting there— he'll be out the door in a heartbeat. Where was Dad, anyway?

When we entered the dining room, I was shocked to see a candlelit table set for two. I guess I wasn't so clever after all. I'd been had!

Mom's favorite declaration flashed through my mind, and I pictured her standing in the kitchen, wagging a finger in my face. *"You have to get up pretty early in the morning to outfox this fox."*

Well, I was getting up early—but apparently not early enough. I jutted my jaw forward and stared my mother down. She pretended to be too busy to look in my direction. When I finally got her attention, she had a smirk on her face. She winked at me and left the room. This was the last straw.

Shortly after, she served the first course of soup. Sammy's eyes lit with delight when she placed a bowl in front of him.

"All right, Mrs. P.," he said. "This is my favorite soup."

"You two enjoy yourselves," she sang.

I glared at her. Subtlety is not one of my mother's attributes. I grumbled under my breath. The woman had no mercy when it came to getting what she wanted. But Italian Wedding Soup?

She knew I'd be upset, but do you think she'd look my way again? Not a chance. She got her message across loud and clear, and Sammy was enjoying the ride with her.

I rushed through the rest of the courses with record speed. I was tired of the small talk, and I wasn't planning to hang out any longer than was necessary. When dessert was placed in front of us, I waited for Sammy to finish his last forkful of tiramisu, and I jumped up. "Okay, I gotta go now. It was nice meeting you, Sammy."

He opened his mouth to speak; I quickly interrupted. I wasn't about to give him an opportunity to ask me out on a real date. "I have a big day tomorrow—."

Mom looked at me in horror when I passed her in the hall. Now it was my turn to give her a smug look. She was speechless. I winked and closed the door behind me.

Relieved I'd done my "penance," I sped out of the building and into my car. While I drove back home, I giggled, thinking about the conversation Megan and I would have tonight about how I outfoxed the fox.

Chapter Six

Over the next couple of months I'd begun to feel more comfortable with the job and developed a regular routine. Each week that passed, I was getting to know more about my boss's likes and dislikes. Besides the heavy workload from Barry, I was also dealing with a backlog my predecessor left behind. Free weekends became a rare commodity, and the euphoria I once felt had faded somewhat. Working the extra hours was part of the job, but the long commute was killing me.

I was tired and rarely had time to file things properly. I had hoped Victoria could lend a hand, but Barry's Type A personality kept her just as busy. Because I was such a perfectionist, the mess on my desk was driving me crazy. Fortunately, I'd managed to wrangle a small table for my office as well.

On my way into the office one Friday morning, I told myself that, no matter what, I was taking the weekend off. Just saying those words gave me a sense of relief. I entered the reception area and passed Victoria's desk.

"TGIF," I said enthusiastically. She was knee-deep in whatever she was working on and simply waved a hand in the air when I walked past her. I'd stopped for coffee and a doughnut at Starbucks. With my briefcase in one hand, I balanced the doughnut on the lid of my coffee container in the other. I could hear my phone ringing, and I rushed into the office. I carefully placed the container on my desk and reached over to push the speaker button. Unfortunately, my outstretched arm knocked over the container, causing an avalanche of coffee to run down the sides of my desk while the doughnut took flight. In my haste I forgot about the phone call and concentrated on the coffee, using my hands as a shield to prevent it from spilling all over me.

"Oh, swell, isn't this just terrific," I muttered.

"Excuse me?" a voice on the speaker said sarcastically.

"Yikes! Hello?"

"What's going on over there?" he said abruptly. "The boss is out, so everyone's having a good time?"

"Barry? Sorry." He sounded furious. "My coffee spilled when I rushed to get the phone. No one's having fun." I changed the subject. "Is there a problem?"

"Problem? I'll tell you what my problem is—*you're* my problem."

"I am?"

"You screwed up royally."

The tightness in his voice made me feel as though his hand was closing around my neck, choking every last ounce of life out of me.

"Tell me what happened."

"You misspelled Kinsey-Clark's name on the slides. You spelled it *Karsey*-Clark."

"Are you sure? I went over everything with a fine-toothed comb."

"Am I sure? What kind of question is that? Do you think I'd be this upset if I wasn't sure?"

"I'm sorry. I didn't mean it that way. It was just a figure of speech. I checked those slides over so many times, it's hard to believe, that's all."

"I'm the laughingstock at the biggest industry conference of the year."

"I understand you're angry, but do you have to be so rude?" I was developing an attitude that was increasingly difficult to keep in check.

"Your screwup gives me the right," he snapped. "After my presentation, the CEO of our company, Dan Rafferty, cornered me. He was very upset and informed me that I needed to pay closer attention to the people I hired. How do you think that makes me look?"

"Well, it doesn't make *me* feel good. But I don't think screaming at me is going to solve anything."

He continued. "If Rafferty was that upset, what about the customer? I looked over at Mr. Clark when I noticed the error, and he was clearly annoyed. We had new customers at this conference. What if they thought about using his service but weren't able to speak to him before they left the conference? How would they locate him if they didn't even have the correct spelling of his company? Your carelessness placed several people in jeopardy, including yourself."

My nerves were flaring. "You know, you might want to consider that there were other employees involved in the process too. How many people on your staff looked at those slides before they left this building?"

"That is not the point, and you know it. It was your responsibility to find those errors before the slides were given to me. You know how hard we're working to win the Jamison account. I used the Kinsey-Clark account as an example to demonstrate to Jamison Pharmaceutical how we increased their profit, hoping to land a deal before I left this conference. Those numbers were also incorrect, by the way. If we can't get the spelling and amounts accurate, does that help our reputation or make the customers believe we're the right firm to represent them?"

"I'm very sorry."

"That's not good enough."

"Well, then, tell Mr. Rafferty I take full responsibility."

"Fine. I'll do that. You know, when we first met, you told me you wanted to advance in the business. Trust me, this is not the way to get ahead."

"Okay, Barry. I get it. I can assure you this won't happen again."

"Well, it better not! As a vice president of this company, I'm expected to be only a little less than perfect, and that includes you as well. This type of behavior is unacceptable."

I willed myself to calm down. He was my boss, after all, and allowed to reprimand me. Under fire, though, I did what anyone would do. I defended myself. Probably not a good thing, since I was relatively new to Merrill.

"I understand. I'll be more careful."

"You do that."

We ended the conversation.

I sat at my desk for what seemed like an eternity, distressed over the typos. The more I pondered the situation, the more I realized the time had come for the big move to the city. Sheer exhaustion was the only viable explanation as to how I'd missed the errors. When it came to my job, I was a perfectionist.

"That's it! I've had enough!" I shouted, slamming a hand down on my desk. "I can't keep putting hours in like this and expect to perform my job well."

Despite the recent chastising, I liked working for Barry. I'd actually begun to think I was liking it a little too much. I reached for the phone and dialed Megan's number.

"Good morning. Born, Bittle, and Bock. This is Megan O'Malley."

"Hi, Meg, it's me."

"Hey, what's wrong? You sound down."

"I made a whopper of an error on my boss' latest presentation, and I sort of lost my cool on the phone with him. I tried to control it, but he was screaming at me."

"Uh-oh, the Italian temper came out of hiding, huh?" She sighed. "So you'll be more careful next time. I think you'll be fine. From all the things you've told me about him, he'll be okay by Monday."

"That's if he doesn't fire me when he gets back." I blew out air to relieve the tension.

"Stop thinking like that. He's not going to fire you."

"I hope you're right. Do you have anything planned for tomorrow?"

"No, but I'd like to. What'd you have in mind?"

"I thought we could apartment-hunt. After this, there's no doubt in my mind that the time has come. If Barry fires me, I'll just have to look for another job, but I don't want to wait any longer. I'm exhausted, and I can't afford to make any more mistakes."

"That sounds terrific. Hey, I'm ready for this move."

"Well, one of the guys here, Jason Reed, told me when I was ready to make the move to call him. His brother is a realtor. I'll try to get an appointment."

"Good. Then I say let's go for it." She let out a yelp. "You've just made my day, Cass! Okay, I've gotta run—El Bosso just walked down the hall. Call me with updates."

"Will do. Thanks for cheering me up, Meg."

"You're welcome. Hey, take a few deep breaths. You're not going to get fired."

Megan always made me feel better. My anxiety

began to wane, and the prospects of moving to the Village became even more appealing. Another one of my dreams was coming true.

"Hey. Cassie. Hello. Knock, knock," Victoria said, as she pounded her knuckles on my desk. "Anybody there?"

She startled me. I was so engrossed in self-pity, I hadn't noticed her standing in front of me.

"Boy, you're sure deep in thought. What's going on? You had the strangest look on your face. Are you okay?"

"Yes—no, I don't know . . . I guess so. Barry just called me about some typos in his presentation. He was so mad at me."

"He is a stickler, but, knowing Barry, he's over it already. Trust me, he'll be fine. He yells and gets it off his chest, and five minutes later he's as sweet as pie. That's the nature of the beast. Know what I mean? Stop worrying. We all make mistakes," she said, scrunching up her face. "Next time you'll pay closer attention."

"Thanks. Megan said the same thing."

"You look as though you could use a cup of coffee. Let's go to the cafeteria."

"Now, that sounds like a great idea. I'm such a flippin' klutz, I knocked over my coffee trying to reach for the phone, and it spilled all over my desk."

She chortled. "I wondered what that squeal was all about."

We stepped into the elevator, and I began to think about searching for an apartment. "Hey, want to hear some good news?"

"What? Tell me."

"Megan and I are going apartment-hunting tomorrow—that is, if I can get an appointment with Jason's brother."

We walked into the cafeteria, where several employees stood in line at the coffee station. Victoria turned to me and nodded. "Speak of the devil, there's Jason."

"Hey, Jase, how are you?"

He walked over to us. "Hi, ladies. It's nice to see you looking this chipper so early in the morning."

"You too, Jase," Victoria said. "How are things in your department?"

"Things are going well," he said with confidence. "Cassie, I haven't seen you in a long time. You must be hiding in that office of yours," he said with a smile. "You know, all work and no play makes for a dull girl."

"I'll say!" I answered emphatically. "Yep, Barry keeps me hopping." I sighed. "I'd like to stop by your office later—will you be around?"

"And the purpose of your visit would be . . . ?" he teased in a deep voice.

"I'd like to see if I can get an appointment with your brother for tomorrow. I know it's last-minute, but I need to do something. The hunt is on for an apartment."

"I'll give him a call when I get back to my office. But wait, I've got a better idea. Let's have lunch today. That will also give me plenty of time to convince you to accept *my* offer."

"Hmm, that sounds ominous. Accept what offer?"

"Aha! I've piqued your curiosity!" he exclaimed with pleasure. He looked over his shoulder as he walked away and said confidently, "See you at twelve-thirty."

Victoria faced me and asked, "What was that all about?"

I shrugged. "I haven't a clue." I watched him walk away. "Boy, he sure is a cutie-pie, though, isn't he? I just love being around all these young executives."

Chapter Seven

"Oh, Cassie. Where did you put the dumb file?" I yelled aloud, shuffling through the papers on my desk, searching for notes from a meeting I'd had with Barry about the Jamison account. Frustrated for not being more careful about where I placed things, I chastised myself. "I'm such a dingbat these days." I spotted a yellow file folder in a stack on a corner of my desk. "Oh, wait. Here it is," I said, relieved.

"You are hysterical, Cassie."

Startled, I turned to see Jason standing in my office. He began to laugh. "Do you always talk to yourself like that?"

"I must be losing it. I never even heard you come in. Is it twelve-thirty already? And how long have you been standing there watching me have a hissy fit?" I asked in a series of questions.

"Oh, I'd say long enough to know you need to be better organized."

"Hey, watch it, buddy. I'm organized. I just misplaced *this* file," I said, holding it up for him to see.

"Yeah, I can see that," he said with a smile on his face.

"All right, wise guy. I know my desk is a mess. I've been working too late, and I'm too exhausted to clean it at night."

I began organizing the papers into neat piles, feeling slightly embarrassed that my office was such a mess. I actually hadn't realized how bad it looked until he mentioned it.

"Okay. But is it necessary to do that right now? I'm awfully hungry."

"Yeah, but now I feel like I've gotten caught with my hand in the cookie jar." I chuckled.

"Nah. You just need to move to New York, that's all."

"There you go," I said, pointing. "But then, that probably means I'll be spending more time *here* if I live closer." I stopped fussing with the stacks. "Speaking of which, did you have a chance to talk to your brother?"

"I did." He reached for my hand and pulled me away from the desk. "I'll tell you on the way to lunch."

"Okay, okay, I'll stop." I walked behind my desk and pulled open a drawer to grab my purse. I saluted him. "I'm ready, chief."

"Finally." He held the door open, and we exited my office.

"So? Where are we off to?"

"The new bistro around the corner, if you're game."

"Sure. I've heard several people mention it. It sounds like a nice place for lunch."

We left the building and walked the few blocks. The weather was so glorious, I removed my jacket. We walked past several office buildings. Granite sidewalks surrounded the entries, and it seemed as though each building tried to outdo the next when it came to potted trees and flowers. The sweet scent filled my nostrils. Young lovers sat eating lunch on the stairs of the office buildings. We continued to make small talk about the weather until we reached the eatery.

"Good afternoon," the hostess said. "Two for lunch?"

"Yes, please. We'd like a table in a corner, if it's available," Jason said.

The hostess, a young woman garbed in the Goth style, picked up two menus and led the way. Her hair was dyed jet black with pink spikes scattered about. She had three visible piercings—one in an eyebrow, one in her nose, and another in her lip. Jason looked at me and made a face. In a low voice he whispered, "Do you see all that jewelry hanging off her face? How can anyone think poking holes there is attractive?"

I shrugged. When we reached our table, we slid into the booth on opposite sides. "Okay, you've had me curious all morning. What's your 'offer'?"

"I'm going to Ryan Garrett's party next month and was hoping you'd join me."

"Gee, Jason, you made it sound so mysterious. You could have asked me at the office."

"Why would I do that when sitting across from you is so much nicer? This way I have you all to myself."

I could feel the glow of a blush rush to my cheeks.

"Ryan's party is 'the event' of the year—in Merrill land, that is. I wanted to make my pitch before someone else beat me to the punch," he said with a grin.

I laughed. "You silver-tongued devil."

His mouth curled into a smile. "Does that mean you accept my offer?"

"Yeah, I think it will be fun. Thanks for asking." I was feeling a little giddy inside, excited about my first date with someone from the ranks at Merrill. I'm sure he could tell by the look on my face.

The waitress approached with a pitcher of water and filled our glasses. "So what will it be today?" she asked.

We both laughed, since we hadn't even looked at the menus.

"Give us a few minutes," Jason said. She nodded and walked away. That was our cue to open the menus and make our selections.

"Do you know what you're having?" Jason asked.

I nodded and told him my choice. He held up a hand, the waitress returned, and he ordered for both of us.

"Now, about that move," I said. "We've been trying

to hold off so we could build up reserves, but the time has come."

"We?"

I grinned at his question. "We, as in Megan O'Malley and me—my roommate and best friend. She's been working in the city at a law firm on Madison for a while and would like nothing better than to live here, but the high rents were unaffordable on her own. Now that I'm here and making better money, I'm pretty sure we can swing it."

"I'm sure my brother can help you find something affordable."

"Does that mean we have an appointment?"

"You do. He had a cancellation. Ten o'clock tomorrow morning—and I'll pick you up."

"You may not want to do that. We live in Nutley. Why don't we meet you at Penn Station?"

"I really think I can manage driving into New Jersey. Give me directions."

"Trust me." I chuckled and held a hand up like a traffic cop. "You do not want me to do that. I'm directionally disadvantaged."

He frowned, waiting for an explanation.

"Don't ask. I don't want to embarrass myself."

"Okay, then give me the street address, and I'll find you." He changed the subject. "Hey, I have a great idea. Why not plan to stay for dinner after we apartment-hunt? You can spend the night at my place if you want, or a hotel if you prefer."

"Don't forget I'll have Megan with me."

"Does she have a boyfriend?"

"Not anymore. They broke up a few months ago. Why?"

His face softened into a smile. "Great. I have just the guy for her, who just so happens to be Ryan's brother. Will she go on a blind date?"

"I'm sure she will, but tell me more about your friend."

"His name is Ralph, and, as a matter of fact, he grew up in New Jersey."

My eyes opened wide in surprise. "No way. It can't be the same Ralphy Garrett I know." I snickered.

"Ralphy?" He grinned. "So you do know him?"

"Maybe."

He looked puzzled. "I just know there's a story here. Fill me in."

"Megan and I have been friends since kindergarten. We first met on the playground at St. Mary's parochial school. During recess the first day I saw her sitting on the steps, and she was sobbing. I walked over and asked what was wrong. She pointed to Ralphy and told me he was calling her 'fatso.' Funny thing is, this Ralphy was pretty hefty himself. I sat with her for a few minutes, waiting for him to say something. Well, it didn't take him long to begin taunting her again. I told her to sit tight because I was going to fix the problem—and I did. I walked right up to the bully and socked him square in the snoot."

Jason laughed hysterically. "You did not."

I nodded. "Oh, yes, I did."

"Why, you little tomboy," he teased. "Remind me never to tick you off."

I continued laughing between sentences. "He was gasping and sputtering, and then he spit something out. It was a tooth! He clenched his fists, ready to take me on, but one of his friends intervened and pulled him away. He left, but not without giving me a glare. Just to aggravate him even more, I put my hands on my hips and shouted, 'Aw, I'm so scared.' "

"You were a little devil. I'll bet you have brothers, don't you?"

"No. I'm an only child. I had to fend for myself when Mom wasn't around to protect me."

"I can't believe that you, little Miss Petite, would have enough strength to knock out a kid's tooth."

I giggled. "I didn't realize I had that much power behind my punch either. I think the tooth must have been ready to come out. I was only five years old at the time, but, as my dad would say, I was a rough, tough cream puff."

"I guess you were."

"I'll tell you, though, no one ever messed with me or Megan again." I giggled.

"I have no doubt."

"I don't want you getting the wrong impression of me, though, so let me tell you about my humanitarian side."

"I thought this might be coming," he said in a playful voice.

"Once I realized he'd lost a tooth, I felt bad knowing he wouldn't have it to put under his pillow to collect his donation from the Tooth Fairy. So after he walked away, I picked up the tooth and gave it to his friend."

"What a sweetheart." He laughed. "I'm sure that made him feel a whole lot better, don't you think?" he teased. "What a funny story. I can just picture it, as though I were standing on the sidelines, watching it happen."

"Anyway, that's how Megan and I became friends. Shortly after the incident Ralphy Garrett disappeared, and I later learned his parents enrolled him in another private school. So what do you think? Is this the same guy?"

He controlled his laughter. "Well, he did go to a private school, but even if he is the same person, it's been years since kindergarten, and I seriously doubt he and Megan would even recognize each other."

"She's going to kill me if she finds out I conspired to trick her."

"Probably, but we're not really tricking her, are we? I mean, this is a real nice guy we're talking about here. So what do you want to do? Should I arrange a date?"

I pondered the idea for a minute. "Okay, what the heck—it's time they face each other anyway, right? Besides, she's really pretty now."

"Tell me what she looks like."

"She has that healthy, wholesome look—a freckled-faced, Irish brunet with deep blue eyes—and she's the kindest, sweetest person you'll ever meet. Personally, I think Ralph is in for a real treat."

"Then it's a date."

Chapter Eight

Saturday morning arrived, and Megan and I were up bright and early. We couldn't wait for Jason to arrive.

Just as I finished getting dressed, I heard the doorbell ring. I rushed to apply the final touches of makeup and headed out to the living room. Megan had already answered the door.

"Good morning. You must be Megan." Jason bowed, curving an arm in front of him as though he were a knight. "Jason Reed, at your service."

Megan began to laugh and invited him into the apartment. Jason looked adorable in his casual attire. He wore a baseball cap, T-shirt, and jeans.

"It's very nice to meet you, Megan. Cassie has told me such nice things about you."

"She lies," Megan teased.

"Say it isn't so," he teased right back. He noticed me standing there. "So, are you ladies ready?"

"Oh, yeah," I said. "We didn't sleep a wink last night. We're so excited about the prospect of moving to the city."

"Well, then, let's get going," he said.

We left the apartment and got into Jason's car.

We drove into the city and parked in front of Christopher Reed's real estate office. After the formal introductions and a look through the listings, we left with a long list of rentals—none of which was ultimately to our liking. After walking through the fifth apartment, Megan and I looked at each other with disappointment.

She was the first to speak up. "Christopher, we'd like to cut to the chase here. These places aren't working for us. Don't you have anything else . . . like, in the Village?"

"I agree with Megan," I said. "I need to feel a certain warmth when I walk through the door . . . like I'm home."

Christopher rubbed his chin, deep in thought, then raised a finger. "Hmm . . . wait right here while I call a client of mine."

Our eyes opened wide with anticipation.

"What do you think, Jason? Do you think he's going to find something for us?"

"Not to worry. I've never known him to give up the search."

Christopher returned with a smile on his face. "We're in luck, ladies."

"What?"

"I've been dealing with this client for over a week now. He has a place in the Village he's just listed for rent. He's getting married next month, and they've already purchased a house. He wasn't really sure if he wanted to rent out his apartment or keep it as a second residence. He and the future bride decided to rent it out."

"That's super!" I screeched.

"Okay, so let's get into the car and drive over there," he said with a smile. "My client was on his way out, but he said he'd leave the key with a neighbor so we could see it today."

Megan and I jumped with joy. "Oh, how fantastic is that?" I squeezed Megan's hand in excitement.

After a short drive, Christopher pulled up in front of the brownstone. Images of life in the big city and living in a place like this danced through my mind. It was Christmas all over again, and I was receiving my long-awaited gift. Unable to contain my excitement, I shouted, "Oh, Megan, look at this place!"

I got out of the car and stood by the stairs that were sandwiched between wrought iron railings leading to the front entry. I marveled at the architectural details—the building's large windows, hand-carved arched doorways, and huge brown stones.

Christopher picked up the key from the neighbor while we stood waiting. He unlocked the door, and

Megan and I looked at each other, knowing instantly that we'd entered paradise. This was it! This was home.

"Wow! This place is fabulous."

We ran from room to room, shouting "Oh, my God!" to each other as we passed in the hallway.

"Can you believe the size of these rooms?" I said. "Look at that kitchen. Even Lucy Pirelli would be proud of us with a kitchen like that."

Megan laughed. "Yeah. Now all we have to do is learn how to cook."

That got a chuckle from everyone. We continued to examine the rooms and both stopped and looked in awe at the fireplace in the living room. Megan and I glanced at each other and nodded. "This is it, isn't it, Cass?"

"Yep, this is home. Hey, did you see all the cafés and restaurants nearby . . . and did you see the park?" I asked.

"Do you think we can afford it, Cass?"

I turned to look at Christopher. "Can we?"

"Based on both your incomes, I don't see why not."

We squealed with delight, jumping up and down like two children. "Shall we sign a lease today?"

"Bring it on!" Megan shouted excitedly. "I just love this place! Oh, Cassie, I know I'm not going to be able to sleep until we move in here. I'm so excited. Let's go home and pack."

Jason and Christopher laughed as they looked on. "So I guess this is the place, huh?" Christopher asked, chuckling.

"Absolutely. Let's head back to your office and sign the lease."

Jason chimed in. "How about some real New York pizza first? There's an amazing place down the street that has the best. They use wood-burning ovens to bake it . . . it's delicious."

"Well, all right," I said, scrunching up my nose. "But can anyone else sign a lease on this while we're gone?"

Christopher smiled. "I'm the sole realtor for this rental. Mr. Weiss gave me an exclusive on the listing."

Megan and I exhaled simultaneously. "Okay, then, let's go eat."

The two of us talked nonstop all the way to the restaurant, about the apartment and possible decorating ideas. When we arrived at the quaint Italian eatery, it was packed. We joined the long line of waiting customers.

I hadn't realized how hungry I was until my stomach started talking back to me at the aroma coming through the open door. A waiter walked out, holding a basket in one hand and tongs in the other. My vision was blocked by other customers, so I stretched my neck, trying to get a glimpse of what he was passing out. But I couldn't see.

"What is he handing out to those people?" I asked.

"This place makes their own garlic bread. On Saturdays they know the lines will be long, so they make extra to pass out to the customers. That way you won't mind the long wait as much. That waiter will also take our order, so by the time they have a table ready, our food and drinks will be too. How's that for marketing?"

Megan and I said in unison, "Great. I'm starved."

Our turn came, and the waiter escorted the four of us to a corner table. Jason was right. Our food was delivered shortly after we were seated. I bit into my all-time favorite, an eggplant Parmigiana sandwich, and released a loud "Mmm." Jason, Christopher, and Megan got a pizza with everything on it.

"Just think," Megan said, "we can eat here every night if we want. Look how close we are to our new apartment."

"Works for me," I agreed.

After we devoured every last morsel of food, we drove back to Christopher's office to sign the lease and pay the first installment. Once everything was signed, we thanked Christopher and left. I was feeling pretty confident, knowing I had the next phase of my new life tucked under my arm in a manila envelope.

"Hey," Jason said enthusiastically, "since we have time to kill before we meet Ralph, want to walk off our lunch by touring your new neighborhood?"

"Yeah. That would be fun. What time are we meeting your friend for dinner? I'm so full now, I don't know how I'll ever find room for more food," I said.

"I have to call him when we're ready." Jason stopped. He looked at us and said, "Actually, why wait? Why don't we call him now, tell him to meet us at the local coffeehouse, and we can sightsee together?"

I looked at Megan, waiting for her response. She nodded and smiled in approval. Jason took the cue and dialed Ralph's number from his cell phone.

We waited for him at a neighborhood café.

When he walked through the door, I was the first to notice him. I kicked Jason under the table and gestured for him to look up. Sure enough, I was correct. Ralph still had an adorable smile accentuated by deep dimples. Jason stood and made the introductions without mentioning Ralph's last name.

Ralph sat down next to Megan and looked at each of us with a curious frown. Jason and I began discussing work, trying to ignore Ralph's obvious struggle to place us.

I overheard him say to Megan, "You ladies sure look familiar to me. I know I've seen you somewhere. Where do you live?"

Trying to avoid his question, I piped up, "As of today, right here in the Village. Tell us about yourself, Ralph. What do you do for a living?"

He answered my questions, then turned to face Megan. They began talking and seemed to be having a wonderful time becoming acquainted, when suddenly Megan shouted, "You went to school where?"

Ralph looked at both of us and launched into a riproaring fit of laughter.

Megan glared at me and asked, "Cassie, did you know who Ralph was when you set up this date?"

"I—I guess I did," I said meekly. "But I wanted him to see how beautiful you are now."

He stopped laughing. "You're right about that Cassie . . . she is beautiful." In a serious voice he said, "You know, Megan, that day on the playground has bothered me for years. I'm really happy to be able to see you now and apologize for being such a jerk."

Megan looked at him—and her face softened as she touched his arm and accepted his apology.

Pointing to me, he spoke to Jason, "Watch out for this one, though! She has a mean left hook."

Everyone laughed, including me. "Oh," he said to me, "by the way, thanks for returning my tooth. The Tooth Fairy took pity on my swollen lip and left me ten bucks."

Chapter Nine

"**H**ey," Victoria said, as I walked past her desk on Monday morning, "Jensen's Florist delivered a tree for you this morning."

"A what?" I asked. "Did you say a tree?"

"Yep, I did. So who do you think it's from?"

"It has to be my mother. Who else? This must be a new approach to remind me that I've disappointed her by taking this job."

Victoria cocked her head to the left, her brow furrowed in a frown. "Why? What does she have against your working here?"

"We're talking an Italian mama, my friend. She's been spoon-feeding me guilt since I started eating solid foods, so she's probably making sure I don't forget she's upset—about my taking this job, about breaking off my engagement, and, if that wasn't enough, about my adding insult to injury by making her lose a bet with a friend."

"You made her lose a bet?"

I held up a hand. "Believe me, you don't want to know." I lowered my voice to a whisper and pointed toward Barry's office door. "Is he back?"

She nodded and smirked. I smiled and headed down the hall, my heels clicking on the floor along the way. I heard Victoria's voice in the distance.

"Hey, let me know who sent the tree, will ya?"

"Sure," I shouted back. I walked into my office and was amazed by the enormity of the tree. It was huge and took up an entire corner of the room. No way could my parents afford something this grandiose. Puzzled, I reached for the card that was attached to a branch. I no sooner touched the tree, trying to pull off the card, when something slithered across my foot. I let out a bloodcurdling scream. Out of the corner of my eye I saw a tiny snake trying to take cover under my desk. I ran for the door, bumping into Barry, almost knocking him down, and Victoria, who had rushed in to help the damsel in distress.

"What? What's wrong?" they shouted.

I ran toward the door. Clutching my chest, I squealed, "Oh, my God, there's a snake in my office!" I shuddered and ran out into the hallway.

Barry started to laugh hysterically. When he regained composure, he said, "A snake? This is New York, not New Jersey. We don't have snakes here."

"I'm telling you, it's a snake," I said with defiance. "I know what a snake looks like. And that—that *thing* slithered over my foot," I said nervously.

Victoria pointed at my foot. "Ooh, what's that spot on your suede shoe?"

I held on to Victoria while I rubbed the tips of my fingers over the spot. "Oh, yuk, it's slimy—the thing pooped on my new shoes."

Barry laughed. "You see what you did? You scared the crap right out of him."

"Very funny, Barry. These are the most expensive shoes I've ever purchased. I just hope they're not ruined."

Barry eyes scanned the floor. He brought a finger to his lips and whispered, "Shh, I think I see something." He pointed. "Over there." He gingerly tiptoed toward it. As he approached, the snake made a beeline for the corner. "Oh, wow, it *is* a snake." His eyebrows rose in surprise. "Now, how did the bugger get in here?" He scratched his head. "It couldn't have come in with the potted tree, could it?" he said, suggesting the obvious.

"I don't care how it got here. I want it out."

"Okay, go down to my office and wait until Victoria can get maintenance up here to remove it. Let's close the door so it doesn't make its way out into the hallway. I'll have a stampede on my hands if the other women see it."

"So who gave you that beautiful tree?" Victoria asked.

"I have no idea. When I reached for the card, the icky

thing scooted over my foot and scared the daylights out of me."

Barry began to whistle playfully as he walked away, tucking his hands into his pockets.

Victoria and I looked at each other in surprise. She pointed a finger at him, and we shouted in unison, "It was you?"

He avoided the question. "Victoria, make that call right away, and tell them to hurry. I want that thing out of here before it causes any more havoc. Make sure they know what they're dealing with." He shook his head in disbelief. "They're going to think you're nuts when you tell them."

He glanced my way and tried to hold back his laughter at my obvious fright. "Hey, I thought you were a country girl. I'm sure this isn't the first snake you've ever seen."

"Excuse me?" I was angered by his comment, regardless of whether or not he was joking. "I may live in what you call 'the country,' but Nutley is not in the boonies. Nutley is considered a city. Of course, not like New York City but, nonetheless, heavily populated with people, not snakes."

He burst into uncontrollable laughter, bending over to clutch his stomach.

"I do not find this one bit amusing, Barry. That thing scared the heck right out of me."

He held up a finger. "Excuse me for a minute." He

directed his attention to Victoria. "Hey, Vic, while you're at it, call Jensen's Florist and let them know they've just lost a very good account. We're not buying another thing from them, *ever*."

"So it *was* you!" I shouted. "Why would you buy me a tree?"

"Why? Because your office needed a tree, that's why." His grin caught me off guard and made my heart beat faster.

How do you stay mad at someone who's just bought you a tree? The man's going to drive me to drink. "Well, thank you, I guess. That was a nice gesture. But I'd appreciate it if you'd stop laughing at me now."

"I'm not laughing at you. I'm laughing with you."

I pointed to my face. "Do you see me laughing?"

"You're right. Okay, I'll stop." He cleared his throat and looked at me but could not contain himself. His laughter was so contagious, I joined him.

"I'm sorry, but if you could have seen the look on your face—it really was priceless."

"Did you put that snake in the pot as payback?"

The muscles in his jaw tightened. "Certainly not," he said adamantly. "I may be a lot of things, but sinister isn't among them." He held open his office door for me to enter. "Take a seat. I'd like to talk to you."

"I agree. I think we need to discuss what happened on Friday."

He gave me a glance and closed the door. "Are you

okay?" he asked remorsefully. "I really am sorry about the snake."

"I'm okay. Shall I get my notebook for this discussion?"

"No, you won't need to takes notes." He sat down in his chair. "I wanted to discuss the tension that's bound to build between us if we don't resolve this issue. I don't like loose ends, and I don't enjoy reprimanding employees, especially fairly new ones. I admit that my anger was a bit over the top."

"You think?"

His mouth pulled into a twisted smile. "Get used to it, because that's who I am. I say what I have to say and move on. I bought that tree for your office *not*—and I want this clearly understood—because I'm sorry about what I had to say. But I am sorry about the way I handled it. I'd like to get past this and return to developing a solid working relationship. That's what we're going to need if we're to succeed."

"I'd like that too. I really am sorry for not catching those typos. I can only imagine how embarrassed you felt. Did Mr. Rafferty ever cool off?"

He nodded in the affirmative. "He did, but we need to be very careful when it comes to him. Fortunately, I was able to calm him down somewhat." He pursed his lips.

"I'm sorry I shouted back at you too. I really do enjoy working for you."

"I think we'll be able to work this out. It's the newness

of the relationship, getting to know each other, our likes and dislikes, our personal styles. It'll be okay."

"Good. I'm aiming for the same thing."

"All right, then, let's forget it and move on."

"That's a deal. Oh, and thank you for the tree. I really do appreciate your thoughtfulness. Of course, I'm not crazy about the snake, but I guess I should thank the little reptile for breaking the ice."

"How about we go down the street for breakfast to continue our conversation while maintenance does its job?" His face lit up with a boyish smile. "Have you had breakfast yet?"

"I grabbed a Twinkie as I ran out the door this morning."

"Oh, good," he said with sarcasm. "That's certainly nutritious for a woman on the go."

We exited his office just as the maintenance department's Slime Busters headed down the hall. I could hear one man excitedly shouting strategy directives to the others about catching the snake. Barry and I both laughed at their attire.

"Look at those getups, will you?" he said.

All six of them had their trousers tucked inside their boots. Their hands were covered with gloves, and one of them carried what looked like a butterfly net.

"A bit over the top, don't you think?" I chuckled.

Barry glanced at Merrill's finest, then back at me. "I guess they're afraid the snake might crawl up their pants when they least expect it." He released a throaty laugh. "Let's go have breakfast."

"Good, I'm starved. You'll be sorry you invited me." I was relieved we'd had our talk.

Upon entering the restaurant, the hostess escorted us to a table. Barry sat down and released a heavy sigh.

"Are you okay, Barry?"

"Huh? Oh, yes. I was just thinking about something. I'm sorry."

The menus were delivered. While I browsed through the selections, I could feel Barry staring at me. I glanced up and noticed an intense dreamy expression on his face. Whatever he was thinking about, it wasn't work related.

I felt a bit of queasiness develop in the pit of my stomach. I smiled at him for a second, then averted my eyes back to the menu. I shook my head, trying to block out the thoughts I was having. I don't know what's wrong with me. Dating the boss and promotions don't go together. Not that it's an unheard of occurrence, but it wasn't going to happen to this chick. But then, I really didn't want to date my boss anyway, did I? I pondered that for a few minutes. *Yeah, right.* "I don't," I said aloud.

"You don't what?"

"Ah, um, I don't want to have anything too filling," I lied, trying to cover up my outburst.

"I thought you said you were starving."

"Well, I am, but I'm dieting."

"You're what?" he said with surprise. "You're dieting?" He placed his fingers together to form a circle, "Your waist is about this . . ." He stopped in midsentence, and his face flushed with embarrassment. He remained silent for a few seconds, then cleared his throat. "Have you decided what you're having?"

"Yes. You've convinced me I should eat something substantial. I'll have an omelet."

The waitress arrived, and we placed our order.

A sudden serious look crossed his face. In a stern voice he said, "Okay, let's talk." He rubbed his chin. "Tell me about your goals. What is it you want to achieve from this job?"

"My goal is to do the best job I can and advance in my career."

"How important is that to you?"

"Extremely important," I said emphatically.

"Good. I'm asking you because I want you to understand that my goals are just as important to me as yours are to you. While a typo is not the end of the world, having my boss and my customer in the audience was an embarrassment not only to me, but to them as well."

"I understand that."

"I don't know if you're aware of this or not, but I'm going to give you a little background on the relationship I have with Dan Rafferty." He turned to see who was sitting nearby. "Rafferty is resentful of me because I progressed rapidly early on in my career. As you've seen, the executives in this organization are very young. I'm the youngest vice president in the history of Merrill, and he doesn't like it. He feels I haven't paid my dues the way he had to, so whenever something like this happens, it's one more nail in my coffin."

"I had no idea. I'm surprised Victoria didn't tell me."

"You're kidding. You mean there's one thing she hasn't told you?"

I only smiled. I wasn't about to rat on a co-worker, nor did I want him to know the extent of our conversations. "I'm glad you've shared this information with me. It's important for me to know."

"Regardless of whether or not you know, it should make no difference in the quality of work that comes out of our office."

"Of course. That goes without saying. My only defense is to say that I've been working too many hours and commuting too far. That situation will soon be remedied."

His jaw clenched. "So, are we clear on this point?"

"Yes, perfectly clear. It won't happen again."

"The upcoming Dallas conference is especially important to me. Dan will be in the audience again. I know he wants to retire, and I want to be his replacement."

The food arrived, and we began eating in silence. "Will you help me, Cassie?"

"Of course I will."

"So, tell me, what is the 'remedy' you referred to?"

"I'm happy to say I will soon be a resident of the Big Apple, living in the Village."

"That's super. You'll love the Village. Is that what you did over the weekend? Find an apartment?"

"Yes, as a matter of fact. My friend Megan and I will be making the move as soon as we paint the place."

"So now that you're moving here, what will you do with all your free time?"

"Free time?" I rolled my eyes, "What free time? I'm always working—well, not on weekends, but that's when I run all my errands and spend time with my family."

He changed the subject. "So I understand you'll be attending Ryan's party?"

"How did you know?"

"I was having coffee with him the other day when you walked by with Jason, and he mentioned you'd be Jason's guest." He took a deep breath. "So, how long have you two been dating?"

I laughed. "Jason and I aren't dating. He just invited me to the party. He's a very nice man, though."

"Does that mean you'd like to date him?" he teased.

I giggled nervously. "I really haven't given it much thought, to tell you the truth." Floored by his question, I wondered why he was asking—although his spirits seemed light and jovial afterward. It actually was a breath of fresh air to see him so relaxed.

"So, how did you find an apartment in the Village

so quickly? Those rentals are usually hard to come by, because no one ever wants to leave once they're in there."

"Jason's brother is a real estate broker."

"Hmm, I see. Jason again, huh?"

I giggled. "It isn't what you think. Really, it isn't."

"I didn't say anything."

"Yeah, but the look on your face did."

"Hmm," he said, rubbing his chin. "I'm that transparent, huh?" He looked amused. "Well, I think this will be a good move for you." He tilted his head. "I hope you realize it means you'll be able to spend more time at the office."

"That's just what I'm afraid of, Barry."

"I'm only teasing. Let me know if I can help on moving day."

"Wow, thank you. That's a generous offer, but I'm sure you have more important things to do on the weekend."

"Actually, it would be a nice diversion for a change—so let me know when you plan the big day."

We finished breakfast and headed back to the office. When we walked into Victoria's office, she was on the phone.

"I wonder if maintenance caught the creepy-crawly thing," I said to Barry.

Victoria finished the call and looked up at us. "Did you two have a good breakfast?"

"We did. Did maintenance find the snake?" Barry asked.

"Yes, thank God. They had a tough time, but it's gone, and Cassie's office is back to normal."

"That's good. I have a ton of work to do." I turned to face Barry. "Thank you for breakfast . . . and the talk."

"You're welcome." He turned to leave, and Victoria called out to him.

"Barry, Mr. Rafferty was here to see you. He asked for you to call when you returned."

His face looked a little ashen. I stood with my mouth open in surprise, wondering what Dan Rafferty wanted.

Chapter Ten

"Do you have a minute?" Victoria asked, standing in the doorway of my office. "I have to tell you something."

"Ooh, that doesn't sound good. If it's bad, forget it," I said in jest, motioning for her to have a seat. "Come on in and sit down. What's up?"

Her face was grim. "You're not going to believe this."

"Try me."

"I'm only telling you this because I know how important this job is to you."

"Okay. Go on."

"There are lots of rumors flying around."

"Rumors?" I placed my elbows on the table and cradled my chin, waiting for the bomb to drop.

"How's the presentation coming along?" Victoria asked me.

"Victoria," I said firmly, "get to the point of this visit. You've piqued my curiosity, now spill your guts."

She leaned forward in her chair and whispered, as if someone might hear her, even though the door was closed. "I wanted to give you a heads-up."

"About what?"

"What's being said about you and Barry."

"Me and Barry? What are you talking about?"

"Janet Smith, Dan Rafferty's secretary, pulled me aside this morning when I went down for coffee and tried pumping me for information."

"Information about what?"

"About you and Barry. It seems people are beginning to wonder what your relationship is with him."

"What? Why would they wonder that?" I shook my head. "Hello? The man's my boss, people."

She took a deep breath. "Did you walk through the cafeteria with Jason the other day?"

"Yeah. So what?"

"Well, she said Barry was sitting in a corner, watching the two of you, and he looked quite distraught."

"That's absurd. She must have misread his expression. It's only been a few weeks since I screwed up on his presentation. I'm sure it had something to do with that. He was probably wondering why I wasn't in my office working."

"Janet said he was ogling you."

"What? Oh, puh-leeze," I said, laughing at the absurdity. "Give me a break." I shook my head in disbelief.

"You know what a gossip she is. And why are you listening to this crap, anyway?"

"I know she's a gossip, but, quite honestly, I've noticed the way he looks at you too."

"Please stop. This is ridiculous. You ladies need to get out more. You've been reading way too many romance novels."

Victoria's eyebrows arched, and her face took on a stern expression.

"I think Janet's on a fishing expedition, looking for something she can tell Rafferty, who obviously put her up to this," I said.

"And I think you need to get your head out of the sand, my dear. I also know a lusty look when I see one."

"Forget it. It's all in your head. You and I both know what the company policy is on dating subordinates—immediate dismissal. Besides, I don't have any interest in dating my boss."

"Uh-huh." She nodded. "Sounds to me like you've been reading up on the subject."

Puzzled, I said, "What is that supposed to mean?"

"I've seen the way you look at him too."

"You're being ridiculous." My heart took a nosedive when I recalled Barry's question about Jason and me. Maybe she was right.

"What? You have a strange look on your face. What are you thinking?" Victoria asked me.

"Well . . ." I scratched my head. "Hmm . . ." I debated whether to tell her about Barry's questions about

Jason. "Nevermind, it's nothing," I said, deciding not to reveal anything to her. We're friendly at the office, but I'm not about to chance her repeating it to someone else—like Janet Smith.

"Cassie, it's okay. You can tell me. I won't tell anyone." She crossed her heart with a sweeping motion of her fingers. "I promise never to repeat it." She grinned mischievously. "I think it would be wonderful. You two would make a great couple."

"Stop it, Victoria. It's out of the question, and there's nothing going on." I raised my voice. "Spread that around, will you? We need to squash this rumor before Dan Rafferty makes it into a major problem and something else to hold over Barry's head." I took a deep breath. "Stop and think about this for a minute."

"Okay, I'm thinking."

"Seriously, knowing Barry isn't well liked by his boss, can you honestly believe he'd be foolish enough to buck company policy for the sake of a woman? He wants a promotion, and Rafferty would use anything he could get his hands on to send him on his merry way."

"That may be true, but when you're in love, company policy takes a backseat. Get real, Cassie! He's interested, all right, and the sooner you wake up and smell the coffee, the better off you'll be."

"Maybe he's concerned that I'll leave the company after he's trained me. You know how these executives are. They're so afraid female employees will leave to have babies after they've spent time and money to train them. I don't know, but there's got to be a more plausible explanation than what you're reading into this."

"You have a lot to learn about men." She raised her eyebrows. "And you can't tell me you're not attracted to him. I see it in your eyes every time you're together."

"Well, there's no doubt I think the man is gorgeous, and I won't say I don't enjoy the scenery when he's around—who wouldn't? He's easy on the eyes. But attracted to him? I think not."

"I think you're in denial."

"Stop," I said, holding up a hand. "We are so done with this conversation. I'm at Merrill for one reason, and that's to advance my career."

"Okay," she said, her voice resigned. "If that's the way you want it. But you're only fooling yourself."

"That's exactly the way I want it." I gestured her toward the door. "Out! Go start trouble somewhere else."

"Okay, I'm going." She paused for a moment. "Hey, isn't tomorrow moving day?"

"Yes, and I'm hoping to get out of here early this afternoon. I have a busy weekend ahead, so leave"—I pointed toward the door—"and let me get my work done."

Chapter Eleven

"Look out, Meg!" I shouted. "That box is going to fall on your head if you don't get out of the way." She lurched forward, moving to the left of the box.

"This moving stuff is exhausting, isn't it?"

"I'll say," she said, her voice filled with excitement. "What time did Jason say they'd be here?"

"He said early. I don't know what that means, but I'm sure they'll be here soon. We should make coffee. Do you want to run to the store and pick up bagels or something for them to munch on before they begin to move the boxes out?"

"I'm way ahead of you. I picked up bagels and cream cheese early this morning, while you were still in bed sleeping like a baby."

"You did? I'm impressed." I chuckled. "Aren't you the domestic diva?"

"No. I just have good manners," she mocked. "Just think. Tomorrow morning we can have breakfast at Soranno's pastry café and feast on croissants and lattes. Won't that be wonderful?"

"Yes, it will. I don't want to become a croissant junkie, though—unless they're filled with chocolate. But the genes I've been born with can't take too many occasions of gastronomic excess."

"Hey, with all the work we're doing today, I think we can afford the luxury of eating *two* croissants and it wouldn't matter. We're burning lots of calories."

I groaned. "Isn't that the truth?"

Jason and Ralph opened the door and walked in, bursting with energy. Ralph held up a bag and said, "I have coffee and bagels here."

I turned to Megan and laughed. "You two are so made for each other."

She walked over to hug him. "Thank you, Ralph. That was very nice of you. Cassie's poking fun at us because I was up early this morning and picked up bagels too."

"There you go. You know what they say about great minds. . . . See? That's why I enjoy being with you so much."

Megan blushed and hurried behind the counter to find paper plates.

"Okay, let's dig in," I said. "Thanks to you guys, we'll have something to munch on for the rest of the day."

Jason was the first to finish his bagel. "Hey, guys, we'd better get our butts in gear, or we'll be here until the wee hours of the morning."

"Okay, you slave driver," Megan said playfully. "If we all carry boxes out, we'll get done a lot quicker."

"No. Leave the boxes for us. It's not worth your getting hurt," Jason said.

"What a guy," I said.

An appreciative smile crossed his handsome face, and he and Ralph began to carry the boxes out to the truck. By eleven everything was packed and ready for us to head to the city. Megan and I both drove our cars, packed to the brim with hanging clothing.

An hour later Jason pulled up in front of the new apartment. Megan and I were already inside, looking around the place in awe.

"Can you believe it?" I said. "We've finally made it." I tilted my head back and closed my eyes. "I want to savor this moment forever. This is such a big deal."

"It is," Megan said as she danced around the room on tiptoe. "We're going to love living in the Village."

Jason walked through the door carrying two boxes.

"Aren't they heavy?" I said, rushing to help him.

He laughed. "I think I can handle it."

"Okay."

A half hour later I looked at the pile of boxes that were accumulating faster than we could unpack them.

"How can we possibly have so much stuff? Do you think we'll ever get this all unpacked?"

Ralph walked in; beads of sweat ran down his cheeks. "Do you ladies have anything cold to drink?"

"We do. Hang on for a second. I'll get something out of the fridge." Megan soon handed him a cold drink. "Jase, want one too?"

"That would be nice."

"Cassie, how about you? Want anything?"

"No. I'm good. After we're all done today, I've planned a little celebration with hot hors d'oeuvres—if I can get the oven to work—and some chocolate-dipped strawberries."

At the mere mention of the word *chocolate*, Megan started laughing. "Are we feeling a little stressed, Cass?"

"Just a tad. Why? Aren't you?"

"A little." She rubbed her hands together. "But I'm not a chocoholic like you."

Jason had a surprised look on his face. "You mean you've been holding back vital information? I didn't know you had an affliction."

"It's more like an affinity," I teased.

We continued unpacking while the two guys finished bringing in the remaining boxes, which were stacking up faster than speeding bullets.

We both turned to the doorway when we heard a

groan. "Where do you want this sofa, ladies?" The two men were beginning to show signs of fatigue.

I pointed to a wall in the living room. "Put it over there for now. We can move it later if we want." I handed Jason a towel for his face. "Okay, it's time for a break, everyone."

Exhausted, the two men plopped down onto the sofa, one at each end, and laid their heads on the cushioned arms, closing their eyes. Megan and I continued to unpack while they rested. An hour later we had the refreshments out and were ready to party. We began making subtle noises so the guys would wake up.

Ralph was the first to pick up his head. "Hey, is it Miller time yet?"

"No," I said, "but it is snack time, and we have cold Perrier."

"Okay," he said, disappointed. "I really wanted a beer, but if you think Perrier is appropriate, we'll do Perrier."

Jason pretended to be asleep, but the smile on his face was a dead giveaway.

"You can open your eyes now," I said.

"I can't open them, Cass. They're glued shut."

I walked over with a cold drink. "C'mon, let's party. We've earned it."

He sat upright, rubbed his eyes, and released a heavy sigh. He was holding a hand out, waiting for me to give him the drink, when the doorbell rang.

Puzzled, I looked at Megan. "Who could that be? Our first guest?"

She shrugged. "I don't know. Maybe it's a neighbor who wants to meet us?"

I walked into the entryway and opened the door. A short, stocky young man stood with a basket in his hand. "I have a delivery for Cassie Pirelli."

"You do? Well, isn't this a nice surprise." I accepted the gift package and reached into my jeans pocket to pull out a dollar to hand him. I walked to the kitchen, placed the basket on the counter, and removed the card. Megan immediately started looking through the cellophane to examine the contents and started to laugh.

"There's no doubt this is the work of Lucy Pirelli," she said. "Look at the contents. Scarliotti Brothers tomato-basil sauce, a box of linguine, coated almonds, a box of Italian chocolates . . . and that's all I can see." Her laughter continued. "Hurry. Read the card."

"Hey, I'm dancing as fast as I can." I removed the card from the envelope and shook my head in disbelief when I read it. "Man, I'm going to kill the woman." I handed the card to Megan.

She snickered. "There's no other woman in the world as foxy as your mother."

I rolled my eyes.

"Hey!" Jason shouted. "Don't leave us in suspense. Who sent the basket?"

"My mother's friend Sam."

"I take it you don't like this friend?"

"No, I don't and I wish this friend would leave me alone."

Ralph turned to Jason. "Sounds like you have some competition, buddy."

I responded quickly. "There's no competition."

"Well, that's good. I don't want anyone cutting in on my girl."

"Oh, Jason, stop."

"I obviously have something to worry about if this guy's sending you a gift basket."

"Why should that bother you? We have an agreement, remember?"

"What agreement is that?"

"Jason," I said, "you know very well what agreement."

He looked at Megan and winked. "Oh, you mean the one where we're just good friends? Is that it?"

"That's the one."

He shrugged. "Well, a guy can hope, can't he?"

I continued serving the refreshments and looked at Jason when I heard him whisper something to Ralph and Megan.

"There's nothing to hope for. You should be dating other women," I heard Megan reply.

"Perhaps, but I really only have feelings for one."

"Good. Who is she?"

"She's a cute little Italian about five-feet two, with long dark hair and the darkest brown eyes you've ever seen that sparkle when she smiles. . . . She's as cute as a bug's ear."

I giggled and played along. "She doesn't sound like your type."

"Well, she is, but she doesn't think so yet. She keeps telling me she wants to be friends, but I'm not giving up on her just yet."

I rolled my eyes.

Chapter Twelve

"Cassie!" Barry called out when he saw me walking past his office on my way to the copier.

I stopped. "Hi. How are you?"

"I understand you moved into your apartment over the weekend."

"I did, and I'm exhausted. It's going to take some time to unpack and find a place for everything, but we can do that a little at a time."

"I'm disappointed you didn't take me up on my offer to help."

"As it turned out, I had more than enough help."

"Oh, okay." He flashed me a look of disappointment. "Will you still be attending Ryan's party, since you're knee-deep in boxes?"

"Absolutely. I wouldn't miss it. That's all anyone can

talk about, and I'm really psyched. Will you be there?"

"Yes. I always look forward to Garrett's parties. He and Janice are wonderful hosts."

My heart fluttered in anticipation of seeing Barry outside the office environment at a social event.

"If you think the staff has a lot to say now about Ryan's party, just wait until afterward. This party will be the topic of discussion for weeks to come." He raked his fingers through his hair. "Well, I think I'm going to call it a night, and you should do the same. You've been putting in way too many hours lately— you need a break. See you at the party." He waved and walked out.

"Oh, man! This croissant is so good. Want half, Cass?" Megan said, devouring her pastry while we sat at an outside table at Soranno's. "This place is hazardous to our waistlines."

"Hush. Don't remind me. And, yes, I do want half, but only if you'll have half of mine. Mmm, loaded with chocolate."

"Of course," she answered quickly. "I just love living here, don't you? It's such a treat being able to walk a couple of blocks to the best bakery in New York for breakfast."

"I agree." I resumed eating. "I am glad we waited a week to have these wonderful treats, though."

"Well, I'm not," Megan announced with a pout. "I've been craving these all week long."

"Yeah, I know. Hey, I'm so glad Ralph invited you to the party."

"Me too."

"Did he say anything to you about how we're getting there?"

"Yes, he said they'd be here to pick us up at seven."

"So tell me, how do you like him?"

She gave me her best Cheshire Cat grin. "He's really awesome, Cass. I'm afraid I'm pretty infatuated. I'm not sure what he's feeling, but I hope it's the same. She shook her head. "The chubby school bully." She chuckled. "And now that bully is like a Koala bear."

"What a perfect description. And I think he likes you a lot."

We finished breakfast and paid the tab. "Hey, what are you wearing tonight?"

"Let's go shopping for new outfits today," Megan said, her big brown eyes wide with enthusiasm. "What do you say?"

"Sounds like a plan to me. Barry just gave me a bonus check, so I'm flush this week."

"Well, maybe you'd like to buy outfits for both of us then, huh?" she teased. "Just kidding. Shall we take a cab or walk?"

"Actually, Meg, I'd like to walk. I'm not getting much exercise these days."

"Okay, walking it is. Hey, are we going to the Family Fest tomorrow?"

"Yes, I think we need to. At least I do. We haven't

been there in two weeks, and Mom is getting feistier than usual."

We headed down the street, passing the park along the way. It was a beautiful day, the sun was shining brightly, and the park was packed with people taking advantage of the warmth. Joggers and cyclists raced down the path.

We shopped for most of the day. At three-thirty I announced to Megan, who carried a truckload of packages, "We'd better mosey on home to get ready."

"Oh, okay, if you insist. I guess I did enough damage to my credit card for one day."

We hailed a cab for the ride home to help defray the exhaustion from carrying too many shopping bags. Megan unlocked the door to our apartment and dropped the bags onto the floor. I walked to the telephone to check for messages. There was one. I keyed in the code to retrieve it and heard my mother's voice.

"This is your mother. Do you remember me? I guess that high-class job of yours is keeping you busy, since you've been ignoring your family."

I exhaled deeply and rolled my eyes.

"I hope you haven't forgotten your commitment to your father about helping cater the Davis party. He's counting on you. After all, you did promise him," she said. "If it's not too much trouble to ask, call me when you have the time, so I can give you the details you seem to have forgotten."

"Meg, you've got to listen to this message. The woman never ceases to amaze me."

I handed the receiver to her, and she listened, a smile pasted on her face. When she finished, she asked, "Do you want to save this?"

I laughed. "No, I think I've gotten the point."

"You're mother is something else. What catering job is this?"

"Actually, I'd forgotten about it, to tell you the truth. I vaguely remember my father saying something about a woman he calls the dragon lady who wanted to book a party. I guess she booked it." I sighed. "I did promise him, though, so I won't renege. Besides, he's such a sweetheart, it'll be fun working with him again."

We each headed to our bathrooms to shower and dress in our new outfits. An hour later I entered the living room, where Megan sat in front of the television, watching her favorite sitcom. She looked up when she heard me.

"Wow! You look fabulous in that outfit."

I curtsied. "Why, thank you, ma'am. You look pretty good yourself."

She was dressed in a black handkerchief skirt and a black tee studded with a rhinestone martini glass—her new drink of choice. I wore a melon-and-white striped halter dress with sandals.

"Maybe—" I was interrupted by the doorbell. I checked my watch. "Yep, right on time." I opened the door to let Ralph and Jason enter. They simultaneously released wolf whistles.

Jason said, "You ladies look gorgeous." He turned to

Ralph, "You know, we'll have the best-looking dates at the party. We'd better keep a close watch on these two before someone comes along and snatches them right out from under our noses."

"Jason, I swear you must have taken a course in Flattery 101," I said.

"Well, I mean it. You *do* look spectacular."

"Thank you. You're too kind."

He extended his elbow for me to hook my arm through. "Shall we?"

"Yes, let's. I've been hearing so much about this party, let's go see what it's all about."

Ralph piped up. "Yeah, I have to hand it to my brother. He sure knows how to throw a party. This is one event you don't want to miss." He looked at Megan. "Are you ready?"

"Yes, I am."

The four of us talked nonstop during the ride to Ryan's apartment. We pulled under a canopy and stopped in front of an attendant, who promptly opened the car door, extending a hand to assist Megan and me. A second attendant held open the door to the building, and we entered and followed the signs to the elevator. We boarded the elevator and stopped on the fourteenth floor.

Ralph led the way to the apartment and rang the doorbell. A woman dressed in a black uniform and white apron pulled open the door and stepped aside to allow us to enter. I looked around the apartment with amazement. The décor was enchanting. Janice was the first to greet us. She was a pretty woman, tall and slender with long blond hair. She smiled and immediately grabbed Ralph to hug him. It was obvious Ralph and his family had a close relationship. Ryan Garrett was chatting with one of the guests but looked up when we entered and walked over to say hello.

"Hi, guys. Hi, bro," he said, placing an arm around Ralph's shoulders. Ralph made the introductions, since Megan hadn't met Ryan, and neither of us knew Janice. Ryan smiled, "I'm so glad you all could make it."

"Thank you," I said. "We're pretty excited about being here too."

I looked around in amazement at the beautifully decorated home. I'd never seen such opulence before, and I felt as though I'd entered a palace. There were ceiling-to-floor windows that led to a patio with a magnificent vista of the New York City skyline. The apartment was done in contemporary furnishings, and I was blown away by the unusual sculptures studding the space and the paintings hanging on the walls. Never one to hold back my thoughts, I enthusiastically said, "Your home takes my breath away!"

An expression of satisfaction came over his face. "Thanks."

"The artwork is so unusual."

"Janice did it all. They're all original pieces."

I nodded. "Now I'm really impressed. You have a very talented wife."

"Yes, I do." He reached for her hand, brought it to his lips, and planted a kiss on her palm.

"Please make yourselves comfortable. Mostly everyone is out on the terrace, so please eat, drink, and be merry." He gestured toward the tables, "There's food pretty much everywhere, so enjoy, and I'll catch up with you later."

We walked out onto the huge terrace, where a band was just finishing a song. The party was in full throttle. The place was bursting with energy.

Barry stood in a corner, holding a drink. He looked up and smiled when we walked over to say hello to him. His handsome face was reserved, but I didn't miss his look of approval. His blue eyes met mine.

"It's nice to see you on neutral turf," I said.

"Yes, it is, isn't it? So what do you think of this spread?"

Before I could answer, Jason whisked me out onto the dance floor.

"I'm sorry," I mouthed. Barry nodded. As we swayed to the music, he seemed to watch my every move.

Victoria spotted us and walked over. "Hey, I see you finally made it!" she shouted over the music. Jason and I stopped dancing, and he headed off to visit with some friends.

"We did. It feels so good to be out instead of looking at boxes that haven't been unpacked yet."

"I'm sure it does. So where's your friend Megan?"

I searched the room and spotted her sitting with

Ralph and Ryan. I pointed in her direction. "She's right over there." Megan saw me pointing to her, so I motioned for her to join us.

"Victoria, meet Megan."

"Hi, Victoria," Megan said. "I've heard a lot about you."

"Yes, I feel as though I've known you forever too. Cassie talks about you all the time. So nice to meet you." Victoria acknowledged.

Megan agreed, then Victoria looked over at her date, who fidgeted uncomfortably in his seat. "Well, I'd better get back to my beau. He doesn't know anyone here. Come join us when you're done making the rounds."

Megan leaned toward me and asked in a hushed voice. "Who is that gorgeous hunk leaning against the wall? He hasn't taken his eyes off you since we arrived."

"That's Barry."

"Be still, my heart," she said, clutching her chest. "No wonder you're making typos on his presentations. I'd find it difficult to concentrate on my work too." She moistened her lips. "Yum, I'd just be sitting in my office dreaming about that godlike creature all day."

"Yeah, well." I giggled. "It's a tough job, but somebody's got to do it."

Jason snuck up behind us, grabbed my hand, and twirled me around and back onto the dance floor.

I shrugged. "I guess we're going to dance now, Meg. Catch you later."

She headed back to Ralph.

"Having a good time?" Jason whispered in my ear.

"I am. Thank you so much for inviting me."

"I'm enjoying myself too."

We continued to dance the night away, in between visiting with our friends and following Ryan's directive to eat, drink, and be merry. At 3:00 A.M. we were among the last of the stragglers to leave. We thanked our host and hostess and headed down to the lobby to retrieve the car and head for home.

On the short ride back to our apartment, Jason wrapped an arm securely around my shoulders, making me feel a little uncomfortable.

Hmm. What's this arm doing around my shoulders? Maybe I'm just being silly, and he's only trying to be friendly.

I decided not to say anything, because the mood was light and airy, and I didn't want to rain on anyone's parade.

We reached our apartment, exited the car, and walked to the front of the building. Ralph and Megan ran up the stairs to the door, and he stopped and kissed her. I smiled, knowing that was their first kiss.

Jason held my hand. "I had a wonderful time tonight, Cassie. I hope you did."

"I did. What a party. I can see why everyone talks about it the way they do."

Jason brought a hand up under my chin, tilting my head back to lock eyes with me. "Cassie, I really like you."

Oh, no! Please don't let him do this. "Oh, wow, Jason, I don't—" In an instant his lips found their way to mine. His kiss was as tender as a summer's breeze.

Jason stepped back and smiled. "I know you don't want us to be a couple, but I'd really like to spend more time with you, if that's what it's going to take to convince you."

"Actually, I'm really tired. Maybe another time."

His face became serious. "Are you avoiding my question because of Brixler?"

"What? What does Barry have to do with this?" I responded tersely.

"Take it easy. Let me tell you why I asked that."

"I'm sorry. Okay, go ahead."

"I've heard things through the rumor mill about you and Brixler, and I noticed that he never took his eyes off you tonight, not even for a second."

"Oh, Jason, he was probably just glaring at me. He still hasn't gotten over his snit about the errors I made on his presentation."

"Okay, if you tell me that's what it was, then I'll believe you. But I have to say, the expression on his face looked far from angry. I was surprised he didn't bring a date with him. Even though he vows to remain a bachelor, he does date." He shifted uneasily. "So what do you say?"

I avoided his question. "I think it's time to hit the hay. Thanks so much. I had a wonderful time." I stood on tiptoe and kissed him on the cheek.

He smiled and walked away. When he opened the car door to get behind the wheel, I noticed Ralph sitting in the front seat and was surprised that neither of us had noticed his exit. Jason started the engine, and I watched them pull away. I ran up the steps and headed down the hall to Megan's bedroom. I knocked softly on the door. When she didn't answer, I peeked inside; she was already asleep.

"Gee, Megan, I need to talk to you," I mumbled at her. But I decided that no amount of noise was going to wake her after all the martinis she'd consumed. "I guess it will have to wait until morning," I said. I headed to my own bed.

I shut my eyes and was disturbed by the ringing of my cell phone. I reached across the nightstand and checked the screen. Jason's name appeared.

"Hi, Jase, what's the matter? Did you forget something?"

"Yes, as a matter of fact, I did." He released a heavy sigh. "I forgot to tell you that I'm falling in love with you."

In an instant the phone went dead.

Chapter Thirteen

"Cassie, is my presentation ready yet?" Barry's bellow cut the silence, jolting me out of deep thought and back to reality. Startled, I looked up at him when he entered my office.

"Damn, Barry, I'm working on it. I just got back from lunch."

A muscle quivered in his jaw. "How'd you like the party?"

"I thought it was great. Did you have a good time?"

"Yes, I did." His face became serious. "So how soon will it be ready?"

"I'm dancing as fast as I can," I said. "What's the hurry? I thought I had all day."

"You know how important this presentation is to me."

Confused by his sudden angst, I lowered my voice,

hoping to calm him. "Of course I do. You seem extremely tense this afternoon. Are you okay?"

"Yeah, yeah, I'm fine. This is an important meeting, and I want to be sure you'll complete the presentation before you leave tonight."

I raised an eyebrow. "Barry? Has there ever been a time when I didn't complete your presentation on time?"

"No. I'm sorry. Don't pay any attention to me today."

"Well, you can relax. I won't leave until I've finished."

"What a relief. Thanks, Cass. I should have known better." He paced. "I feel like I'm losing control."

"Control of what?"

"I don't know—maybe my life. I think I need a break." He ran his fingers through his thick hair. "Maybe I need a vacation from everything. Okay, I don't want to take you away from your work."

"Are you sure you're okay?"

"Yeah, I'll be fine." He turned to leave. "Hey, do you need a wake-up call tomorrow morning?"

"That's probably a good idea. Who knows how late I'll be up tonight working on this. But just so you'll know, I really dislike all these last-minute revisions."

"I know. I do too, but when a potential customer who's as important as Jamison agrees to attend, you jump."

"I agree. I just hate rushing to redo the presentation after it was already completed."

"Let me have your address, and Charles and I will stop and pick you up on the way to the airport. That will give you time to catch up on your sleep. How does that sound?"

"That sounds wonderful. Thanks." I'd be traveling with Barry again, and I was plenty nervous. Maybe that's why I was snapping at him so much.

"Okay, I'll let you get back to work. Is your address on Victoria's Rolodex?"

"I believe so. If not, come back, and I'll write it down."

He left and headed down the hall. The sound of his heels clicking on the tiles faded as he got farther away.

I worked for several hours after he left, until hunger pangs demanded my attention. I considered calling in an order but decided the fresh air would do me good, so I hurried out of the building and crossed the street to Decker's Steakhouse and ordered takeout. I was so hungry when I returned to the building, I began eating in the elevator. Passing Victoria's desk, our recent conversation about Barry came to mind. As did Jason's comments.

"No," I said firmly. "I can't think about that now. I have a presentation to finish or I'll never get out of here." I groaned. "As it is, I'm going to be like a zombie tomorrow."

A security guard passed by. "Are you all right, miss?"

I giggled. "Yes, I'm fine," I answered, embarrassed.

I finished the presentation at 1:45 A.M. I was ready for some sleep and extremely relieved that we weren't leaving at the crack of dawn. I grabbed the presentation material and my briefcase and headed out the door for the short trip home. I walked into the apartment, hoping Megan would be awake so I could talk to her about what Victoria and Jason had told me. I went to her bedroom door and peeked in. She was deep in slumber, so I headed to my own room.

I removed my clothing, crawled under the covers, and released a sigh of satisfaction. I rolled over onto one side, bringing my knees up into a fetal position, adjusted my pillow, and closed my eyes. I knew it would only be a matter of time before I'd doze off into peaceful bliss.

I woke to the ear-stinging ring of the phone on the nightstand.

"Hello?" I answered in a raspy, morning voice.

"Greetings, sunshine. This is your wake-up call," Barry said softly.

"Ooh, are you always this cheerful in the morning?"

"It's not morning, sleepyhead, it's after noon. And, yes, I am cheerful in the morning. Why? Aren't you?"

"Sometimes I guess. I don't know. It's too early to talk."

"Well, make sure you get out of bed. We don't want to miss our flight, now do we?"

I groaned, "Okay, I'm up." I sat up, moving my legs over the side of the bed. "See you shortly?"

"Right. In about an hour. We'll be in the coffee shop down the street. Don't take too long."

"I'll be there as soon as I can."

"By the way, I took the liberty of picking up a Twinkie for your brunch," he teased.

"Oh, good, that'll save me time." I replaced the receiver and headed for the bathroom.

I stood in the shower and allowed the spray of the water to caress my body. My conversation with Victoria ran through my mind again.

"I have to call Megan," I said, exiting the shower. "She'll know what to do." I dried myself off, wrapped the towel around my body, and dialed her work number. If ever there was a time I needed to speak to her, this was it. I needed her advice.

"Oh, shoot," I said after dialing. "She's probably in that meeting she told me about the other day." I snapped my fingers and waited, hoping she might have returned to her desk during a break or something. It rang several times before the recorded message began to play.

I ran to the closet and pulled out my suit, mulling over how to handle the matter if the situation presented itself. I sat down at my vanity, stared at my reflection in the mirror, and sighed.

"I can't do this by myself," I said, pulling my makeup case out of the drawer. "What am I going to do if it's true? I know that look Victoria is talking about— I've seen it myself," I admitted as I applied the base over my face and smoothed it with the sponge. "He's awfully friendly suddenly. I mean, really, calling me sunshine." I brushed my eyelids with shadow and curled my lashes. "Would I want to date my boss?" I leaned in closer to the mirror and remembered my goals. "The answer to that is a big fat no," I declared. I stared back at my eyes and knew I was lying to myself.

My mind began to play devil's advocate. *You'd date him if you thought you could get away with it, wouldn't you?*

I gulped. "That's enough of this game. I can't think about this now."

My mind wouldn't shut down, and it started singing a childhood song, *Liar, liar, pants on . . ."*

I looked back into the mirror. "Stop this nonsense. You need to get ready to meet your boss."

I dried my hair and quickly slipped into my suit, checking the mirror one last time. "If what Victoria told me is true, what am I going to do if Barry asks me out?" I shrugged and answered my own question. "There's nothing to do. Right?" I rushed into the living room and grabbed my briefcase and made one last attempt to silence my overactive thoughts. This devil's advocate thing was getting out of hand.

The thoughts kicked back in as I pictured Foxy Guy. "Mmm, ever since I laid eyes on him, he's made my insides churn. And the worst part is, I really do enjoy being around him." I groaned. "So why can't I date him? I answered my own question. "Because if I don't get promoted, I'll have failed at proving Mom wrong, and she'll have won."

Suddenly I had a lightbulb moment—well, almost. "So that's it, isn't it? It's the proving Mom wrong thing that's standing in the way. She says I wasn't cut out for corporate life and I wouldn't amount to anything."

I shook my head. "That's not really what she says. She says I should get married and have babies. She tries to control my life. Ah, I let her. Okay, I'm tossing this Barry thing down the dumper. I'm just going to keep my distance."

I snickered. "How, exactly, am I going to do that? I work for the man. But if I don't have feelings for him, then I have nothing to worry about. Right?"

I walked into the living room and glanced at the mirror on the wall there. The expression I had on my face proved less than convincing. The voice of reason failed, and I daydreamed of what it would be like to be held in Barry's strong arms. "Okay, so now I'm worried."

The phone rang, and I ran to pick it up. I didn't bother to say hello, because I already knew who it was.

"I'm on my way, Barry."

"Barry? This isn't Barry."

"Who is this?"

"How soon we forget. I'm disappointed you didn't recognize my voice."

"Please, I don't have time for games. Who is this?" I demanded.

"It's Sammy, Cass. How ya doing?"

"How did you get this number?" I asked tersely. "It's unlisted."

"Lighten up, will you? I called your office, and the secretary gave me your contact number."

"You mean my mother gave it to you, don't you?" I didn't wait for him to respond. "Look, I'm on my way out the door. I have a plane to catch," I said abruptly.

"Okay, I'll make this fast then. How do you like the new place?"

"I like it just fine, thanks."

"When are you returning?"

"I don't know."

"Cassie, what kind of job is this? You don't know when you're returning?"

"In a day or two. I really have go. My boss is waiting downstairs."

"Oh, okay. Let's have dinner on Friday. I'll take you to my uncle's restaurant."

Impatience won out. "Sammy, I really can't. Thanks anyway."

He interrupted. "But, I really li—"

"Look, I have to run." I slammed the receiver back into its cradle, grabbed my purse, and headed out the door for the coffee shop where Barry was waiting with his driver, Charles. On my ride down in the elevator, I removed my cell phone from my purse and dialed Victoria.

"Good afternoon, Merrill Finance Corporation."

"Victoria, I'm going to say this just once. Do not— and I repeat, do not—ever give my cell number to Sammy Scarliotti."

"Whoa! And good afternoon to you too, Cassie."

"I'm sorry. Good afternoon. I didn't mean to sound like Barry."

"Hey, I'm used to it. Everyone seems to be using me

as a punching bag these days. So what seems to be the problem?"

"Sammy Scarliotti. Did you give him my home phone number?"

"I didn't give your number to anyone except your mother, who called earlier. She said she needed to get in touch with you and had tried your cell but didn't get an answer. Then she couldn't remember where she'd put your new home number and asked if I'd give it to her."

"The woman is unbelievable—absolutely unbelievable."

"I didn't realize giving your phone number to your mother was going to be such a big deal, Cass."

"The woman never stops. Okay, I'll handle it, but in the future, if Sammy calls the office, tell him that I'm out and you don't know when or if I'll ever return."

She began to giggle. "Right, Cassie, like I can really say that."

"Well, whatever you have to say, I need to get this guy off my back."

"Is he an old boyfriend?"

"Good Lord, no. He's the guy my mother is trying to fix me up with."

She laughed. "Your mother's a funny lady."

"You only say that because she's not *your* mother. I'll catch up with you later. Barry and Charles are waiting for me in the coffee shop down the street."

"Have a good trip and an even better meeting."

"Thanks. Bye." I ended the call and walked across

the street to the coffee shop. Barry spotted me and took the last gulp of his coffee when I entered. He and Charles stood to leave, but the waitress called out to him, holding up two containers. One was definitely a coffee cup, and the other was a Styrofoam box. "You forgot something, sir."

Barry shook his head and walked back over to her. She handed him the containers, placing one in each hand. Barry smiled at her and nodded, then walked up to me and Charles. "Here's your breakfast."

Charles left to retrieve the car.

The bottom of the Styrofoam box felt warm. "What did you do—have the Twinkie nuked?"

"No." He shot me a smile. "Since this is breakfast for you, I actually ordered you an omelet and a coffee."

His thoughtfulness gave me a warm, fuzzy feeling. His smile gave me palpitations. "Thank you. That was very nice of you," I managed.

"You're welcome." He grinned. "I actually bought you brunch for selfish reasons."

"You did? Why's that?"

"There isn't any food service on this flight, and I didn't want to listen to you whine all the way to Dallas."

Charles pulled around to the front entrance of the coffee shop. Barry opened the door for me. I slid in. The aroma of the food inside the container was tantalizing my taste buds. I was famished. Barry reached into his jacket pocket and pulled out a small plastic bag containing utensils.

"Thanks. I was wondering how I was going to eat this."

"Did you finish my presentation?" he asked.

I sighed. "Barry, you know I did."

"Right—right, I do know that. Okay, where is it?"

"Oh, no. I must have left it at home," I teased.

His eyes opened wide with surprise.

"It's in my briefcase in the yellow folder." I rolled my eyes and pointed to my case. "Be my guest."

"No. On second thought, I'm not going to look at it. I know what it says, and I'm going to trust you."

"Gee, thanks. Why don't you take a deep breath? You're wound up tighter than a steel drum."

"I know. I know. You're right. I just don't want Rafferty making a fool of me again."

"Well, he won't. Trust me. He'll be thanking you."

"I hope so."

I removed the wrapper from the utensils and dug into the omelet. I was glad we were riding in a limo, because there was plenty of room to spread out. I finished eating, closed the containers, and placed them in a small receptacle next to the wineglasses.

"That was wonderful. Thanks for breakfast. I sure don't eat like this every morning. I wasn't kidding about the Twinkie. It may not be the breakfast of champions, but neither Megan nor I cook, so it's the best we can do under the circumstances."

He shook his head in disbelief.

Charles pulled up to the curb at our airline. We checked our bags with the skycap, then walked to the line of people waiting to go through security. Ten minutes later we were sitting at our gate. Barry unfolded his newspaper and began reading the cover story while I sat and people-watched. It didn't take long before we were on the plane, watching the flight attendant demonstrate the oxygen masks. The pilot's husky voice announced our departure over the loudspeaker.

Once we reached the proper altitude, the plane leveled off, and Barry put his head back and closed his eyes. I couldn't help but admire the strong outline of his jaw. He was such a good-looking man. Sitting so close to him, I was tempted to reach out and touch him, but I opted for daydreaming instead. *What the heck am I doing? I can't believe I'm thinking about him this way.*

Shortly after Barry opened his eyes and looked at me. And it was almost as if he'd been reading my thoughts.

Chapter Fourteen

When we landed in Dallas, we exited the craft and headed to the baggage claim area. The carousel began to spin, and when our bags finally reached us, Barry lifted our luggage off the conveyer belt and onto the floor. I snapped my suitcase handle into place, and together we walked out of the terminal to wait for the hotel shuttle.

"Boy, what a long flight," I complained. "I don't know about you, but I'm ready to hit the sack."

"Aw, really? You do realize this time zone is an hour behind New York, don't you? It's really only dinnertime."

"I know, but I can hear the bed in my hotel room calling out my name."

He laughed. "You're a lunatic—you know that?"

"Yeah, I know it." I giggled.

"I was hoping you'd join me for dinner when we get to the hotel."

"That's very nice of you, Barry, but I really need my beauty rest." I stifled a yawn. "I don't think I'd even make it through dinner. My head would probably fall into my plate. Talk about embarrassing."

He laughed at my comment but looked disappointed.

"Thanks for the invitation, but I think I'll rely on room service tonight."

We arrived at the Adams Mark hotel and made our way to the reception desk to check in. I stood in one line while Barry selected a clerk to the left of me. I heard him ask where he could find something to eat, and she directed him to a place down the hall. He finished his check-in faster than I did and asked me, "Are you sure?"

"Thanks, but I'm sure." I nodded. "Have fun, and I'll see you in the morning."

He gave me a wave and headed toward the lounge. I watched him walk away.

A car arrived, and I rode up to the tenth floor and walked down the hall, looking for my room number. I inserted the key card into the door and entered the room, dropped my briefcase on the floor, and parked my luggage in a corner. I promptly disconnected the telephone to avoid any calls and shut off my cell. I kicked off my shoes and flopped onto the bed for a few minutes before I called room service. I wasn't taking any chances. I was going to get a good night's rest if it was the last thing I did. Ultimately, it was the last thing I did, because I fell fast asleep and never woke until morning.

Disoriented, I jumped out of bed and noticed I was fully dressed. As the fog in my head began to clear, I remembered where I was and how I'd wound up sleeping with my clothes on.

"Boy, I was only going to rest my eyes for a second." I giggled. "That'll teach me."

I reconnected the phone and called room service to order breakfast. Then I made a fast trip to the shower and changed before the bellhop delivered my food. I finished eating, grabbed my briefcase, and headed for the conference room to give Barry his presentation.

Walking toward the auditorium, I saw him pacing back and forth in the hallway. When he saw me, he strode quickly toward me.

"Good morning," I said cheerfully.

"Where did you go last night?" he demanded.

I frowned. "I was in my room. Why?" I asked. "What's wrong?"

"I remembered after you walked away that you still had my presentation. I called your room and your cell several times, but you never answered."

"Oh, I'm sorry, but I disconnected the hotel phone and shut my cell off for the night. I passed out on my bed and didn't wake up until this morning. As a matter of fact, I even slept in my clothes."

"Oh," he said with remorse. "I'm sorry I yelled. Let

me have my presentation. I only have a few minutes to read it over."

"Barry, relax. You're going to be fine."

He took the file and walked to a sitting area at the end of the hallway.

I entered the auditorium, which was filled to capacity. That was a good sign for Barry. I did a quick canvas of the room and noticed several familiar faces from a previous conference.

A few minutes later Barry entered and gave me a weak smile. I returned the smile and said, "Break a leg, boss."

"Thanks. I plan to do just that." He stepped up to the podium to begin his presentation. My job at the conferences was to monitor audience reactions and try to discern which of the attendees showed the most interest in Barry's presentation. Those were the people he would spend the most time with afterward to sell Merrill's services.

I spotted Dan Rafferty in the second row, a wry expression on his face. I was hoping it wouldn't make Barry nervous. Barry blew into the microphone to check whether it was working properly, then began to speak. In short order his audience was captivated. Halfway through, though, I noticed his jaw tighten. He looked at me with fire in his eyes. I gave him a quizzical look, wondering if I'd missed something he'd said. My body tensed, and I started worrying that I might have left another typo.

When his presentation concluded, the audience stood and applauded. I quickly left my seat and waited for him in the back room, knowing he was ready to blow up. He wasn't very good at hiding his anger. I heard his feet pounding the tiles until he burst into the room, closing the door behind him. I gave him a weak smile and waited for the bomb to drop. It didn't take long.

"Cassie, you screwed up again!"

"What are you talking about?"

"I told you Jamison Pharmaceutical wasn't ready to inform the audience it was selling off Acumet, and what did you do? You—"

My blood began to boil. "Just a minute, Barry!" I shouted back. He looked at me with surprise. "First of all," I said, pointing a finger at him, "the last discussion we had, you told me to leave that in the presentation because that's what they wanted." Frustrated and disgusted, I grabbed my briefcase and turned to face him again. "And you know what else? You can take this job and stuff it where the sun don't shine. I've had enough."

His face turned ashen when I abruptly turned on my heels and headed back to my room. I slammed the door and sat on the bed, trying to halt the avalanche of tears. I cried for what seemed like an eternity.

When I finally got over my tantrum, I dried my eyes. Convinced this was his screwup, I yanked the file containing the notes I'd taken during our last meeting from my briefcase and scanned them.

"I knew it! I'm so tired of his crap," I said, closing

the folder and jamming it back into my case. I picked up the phone and called room service. This was definitely going to be a chocoholic day. And I didn't care if it was 10:30 in the morning.

A half hour later there was a knock on the door. I looked through the peephole and let the waiter into the room. The phone began to ring, and I ignored it. It stopped and started up again. I angrily marched over and yanked the cord from the back of the phone, then walked a few feet to my briefcase and turned off my cell. The waiter pushed the rolling cart into the center of the room. When he removed the sterling silver domes off the dishes I'd ordered, my eyes lit up, and I looked at him like he was Willie Wonka from the Chocolate Factory. He saw the look on my face and smiled, then pushed one of the chairs over to the table.

"Will others be joining you?" he asked.

"No, just me. Thank you, I can take it from here." I shoved a tip into his hand, and he turned to leave, a slight smile on his face. I guess these guys see it all.

I sat down, placed the napkin on my lap, and dug into the first piece of chocolate. I didn't even moan with delight—I was too angry. I finished the first dessert, a flourless molten chocolate cake. It oozed chocolate with every delectable bite. When I finished that, I embarked on the second, a seven-layer cake. When I was finished with that, I attacked the third. I hadn't known what to expect when I ordered it, but I figured that the combination of caramel and chocolate anything had to be good. That first bite proved me right. I wasn't stopping until I finished all of them. "I'll show that grumpmeister," I said, my mouth full. The more I ate, the angrier I became. Some people drink their troubles away; I have a freaking chocolate fest.

I raised my fork into the air. "Here's to finding a new job—and to my replacement. I hope you have a hard time finding someone as competent as me, Barry." I liked that thought. "Wouldn't that be poetic justice? It would serve him right." Another thought occurred to me. "Yeah, and I hope she's fat, ugly, and doesn't take any crap from you." That struck me as terribly funny, and I laughed hysterically.

Satisfied with my verbal attack on him, I stuffed my face with more chocolate. That's when the first twinge of pain attacked my internal organs. I'd never eaten this much chocolate in one sitting. I dropped the fork and clutched my stomach, rubbing it in a circular motion, hoping to ease the pain and make me feel better. It didn't. Then I got the brainy idea of walking around a little to help my body digest my overindulgent desserts.

When I stood, I felt light-headed, and I hung on to the dresser for support. I began to worry that I'd overdosed and wondered if I should call 911. I moaned in agony. "Man, what have I done?" Waves of nausea churned in my stomach, making me feel as though I was sailing on rough seas—only this ship was sinking fast. I made my way to the bed and lay down. "Maybe I need a little rest."

I closed my eyes, but it didn't make the pain go away. My heart started beating erratically like a bongo drum. Then I remembered that chocolate is loaded with caffeine. I started hyperventilating. "Okay, Cassie, calm down." I doubled over in pain and brought my knees up to my chest, wishing I hadn't been so foolish. I'd thought I was getting even with Barry, but I was the one who was suffering. I was in so much agony, I begged for God's assistance, promising never to eat another piece of chocolate. I don't know why it would matter to Him, but it sounded good at the time.

In an instant He responded, and I was off to the bathroom, making noises like a rock concert gone bad. I was thankful I was alone.

Suddenly, out of nowhere, I heard Barry's voice calling out to me. For a minute I thought I was hearing things, but no, it was definitely him. Oh, no, how did he get in here? I tried to stop the avalanche, but my body wouldn't cooperate.

"Are you okay?"

"Leave me alone. Go away." I heard him mumble something, and he knocked on the bathroom door.

"What's wrong, Cassie? Are you sick?"

I moaned. "Go away. Haven't you done enough already? I'm sick. I've overdosed. My head is throbbing."

"Overdosed! On what?"

"Chocolate."

He started to laugh. "You can't overdose on chocolate."

"Well, I've got news for you, buster—I just did. Now please leave me alone." I started to cry. "This is embarrassing enough."

"Okay. I'm sorry. We'll talk later, okay?"

"No. I'm never speaking to you again. Please, just *go!*" I shouted.

"All right. I'm really sorry about everything." I heard the door open and close.

Production finally stopped, and I felt better, but my head was still throbbing like someone was hammering out the Morse code on it. I turned on the shower and eased my weak body inside, hoping the warmth would make me feel better. I toweled off and pulled my flannel pj's from my suitcase, slipped into them, and got under the covers, falling fast asleep.

I woke up in the darkness and checked the bedside clock. 10:00 P.M. I sat up and switched on the lamp and reached for the remote to turn on the TV.

Remnants of chocolate were everywhere, and reality set in like rigor mortis. I couldn't believe I'd lost control the way I did. Anxiety attacked my sore rib cage and stomach. It felt like I'd been to the gym and performed too many stomach crunches. I glanced over at the chocolate-stained tablecloth and decided I didn't want to look at it anymore. Remembering what I'd done to myself was too painful. I rolled the cart to the door, opened it, and pushed the trolley into the hallway. I was startled when I heard Barry call out to me.

"Cassie?" he said. "Are you any better?"

Surprised to see him sitting, Indian-style, his back against the wall, I closed the door before he could get up. After all, I was no longer employed by Merrill, and he wasn't my boss, so, technically, I could now treat him the way he'd been treating me.

He knocked on the door. "Please let me in. I really need to speak to you."

"We have nothing to say to each other," I said through the closed door. "You can start running an ad for my replacement."

"Cassie, please don't do this. I've been sitting in this hallway for three hours waiting to speak to you. Please let me in."

Guilt tugged at my heartstrings, and I thought it might be nice to see him grovel for a change, so I acquiesced.

"Come back in an hour. I need to get dressed."

"Thank you, Cassie. Can I get you anything to eat?"

"No."

I couldn't believe I'd allowed my vulnerability to show, especially in front of my boss. But, technically, he wasn't my boss anymore. Nevertheless, it was out there in front of God and everybody, and nothing was going to change what had happened. I felt as naked as a jaybird.

I removed fresh clothing from my suitcase and entered the bathroom to clean up. The hour went by quickly, and before I knew it, Barry was knocking at the door. He entered and handed me a container.

"I thought you might want some chicken soup." His mood was docile.

"Thank you." I motioned for him to sit down. I cleared my throat. "I'm sorry you saw me in such a sorry state. I hope the bellhop, or whoever let you into my room—uninvited, I might add—doesn't share the news of my stupidity with anyone attending this meeting, causing you more embarrassment."

"Thank you. It was security who unlocked your door. I lied about our relationship so they'd let me in. I've been worried sick about you. I feel like such a louse."

"As well you should." I wasn't letting him off that easily.

He continued, ignoring my comment. "And there's no need for you to apologize. I'm the one who owes you the apology." He shifted nervously in his chair. "After my outburst I realized I'd forgotten to tell you that Paul Jamison called me on my way out of the office last night and said they'd changed their minds."

I remained silent, allowing him to try to worm his way out of this one. The more I listened, the angrier I became, because of what I'd been through.

"Jamison wasn't sure they would get the price they wanted and decided to wait. When I announced the exact opposite, Jamison's face flushed with anger, but, of course, once it was out, there was no turning back."

He rested his head in his hands as though trying to hide from the truth.

"After you left, a large crowd of prospective buyers surrounded him, trying to outbid one another. Then all of a sudden his frown changed to sheer excitement, and I became the hero—the good guy." He looked away. "I wanted to run after you, but I couldn't, because I needed to work out the deal with the winning bidder."

I sat in silence, waiting for my opportunity. My head was throbbing, but not enough for me to forget the frequency of being terrorized by my boss's abuse.

"That's where I was all afternoon—meeting with customers." He smiled at me. "And you'll be happy to know that Jamison doubled his profit. Now Merrill's the champion, and Jamison is telling the world."

He chuckled. "Dan even came over and shook my hand and said I did a good job. But the real champion here is you, not me. Please forgive me for my outburst— I jumped to conclusions."

I rubbed my forehead with the back of one hand and said, "Actually, I really think it's best if I find another job elsewhere."

A look of panic covered his face. "Cassie, please don't leave," he begged. "I know I've been hard on you, but it's because I've been fighting this . . . this urge inside me."

"What? The urge to make my life miserable? I can't work for someone who isn't supportive of my best efforts. It seems as though I'm not what you're looking for, so maybe—"

Before I managed to say another word, he lifted me up off the bed and into his strong arms, my last words smothered by the warmth of his lips.

His kiss astounded me. Without realizing it, I clung to him and the sweetness of it all.

He reeled back abruptly, as though he'd stunned himself, and stood staring at me, a look of horror on his face.

The impact of his kiss lingered like the aftertaste of a fine piece of Belgian chocolate. I reached up to touch my lips, overwhelmed with emotion and disbelief.

Confused by my own feelings, my mind begged him in silence while my emotions tugged at my heartstrings.

"Oh, no," he moaned. "What have I done?" He stepped back from me. "Cassie, I am so sorry."

In an instant he was out the door.

Chapter Fifteen

"Oh, my God. Oh, my God! I can't believe he just kissed me."

I rubbed a hand across my lips as thoughts of never washing my face again flashed through my mind. I sat down on the sofa, too confused to deal with the aftermath of Barry's passionate kiss. I was in a trance, my head still cloudy from my chocoholic overdose.

I leaned my head back against the cushion and closed my eyes, willing myself to sleep, then quickly opened them when a barrage of thoughts hit me like a ton of bricks.

"How in the world am I going to face the man tomorrow morning? What will I to say to him?" I fretted. "I don't know how to handle this!" Could I simply stand by my hasty resignation and not show up at all?

My heart raced from the aftermath of caffeine. I was tired and desperately wanted to sleep. I lay down on the bed, but restlessness won out. I got back out of bed and flipped on the TV, not to watch but for company.

I adjusted the pillows behind my back and closed my eyes, reliving the memory of his kiss—the softness of his lips pressed against mine, the warmth of his embrace—and my heart fluttered. It was then that I finally admitted I did have feelings for him. No joke. I checked the clock. It was midnight, but I was going to wake up Megan. If I'd spoken to her before this trip, I might not be in the position I was. I dialed her number. After six rings, her voice mail kicked in. I hung up and didn't bother leaving a message.

I sat in bed, resting my head against the pillows. I must have dozed off, because the next thing I saw was blinding sunlight shining on my face. I got out of bed, showered, and dressed quickly. The ache of anxiety returned when I thought about seeing Barry.

I packed my suitcase, paid my bill using the on-screen checkout process, and walked toward the lobby of the hotel. Several businessmen stood waiting, suitcases next to them, for a ride to the airport. A tall man dressed in khakis and a Yankees jacket held up a sign with *Cassie Pirelli* written on it. I walked up to him.

"Excuse me, I'm Cassie Pirelli. Why are you holding that sign with my name on it? I didn't call anyone requesting a ride."

He checked his clipboard and said, "I have a

reservation right here. It was made this morning, by, uh, let's see." His finger moved across the list. "Oh, here it is, Barry Brixler. You know the guy?"

"Yes. He's my boss. Are you picking us both up?"

"Not according to my chart. Maybe he had to leave earlier and wanted to make sure you had a ride."

"Yeah, but I could have used the hotel's airport shuttle. Well, okay, where's your car?"

He grabbed my luggage, and I followed him out to the car. I felt as though I'd been hit by a train. My emotions were working overtime. My head still ached. On one hand I was happy I didn't have to face Barry, yet on the other I was disappointed. I entered the backseat and closed my eyes, temporarily shutting out the world.

The limo pulled up to the curb at the airport. After my bag was checked, I slowly walked to the gate. When I arrived, the passengers were already boarding. I walked down the aisle to my assigned seat and snapped the seat belt into place. I tried blocking out my thoughts of Barry, but he took center stage. I finally dozed off for a short time and woke when I heard the flight attendant offering a beverage to the person sitting next to me.

I reflected on the argument and the kiss and wondered where the situation was headed. I'd already invested too much time in Merrill to throw it all away. And the last thing I wanted was to give Mom the satisfaction of knowing I'd failed. In no time she'd have Sammy Scarliotti camping out on my doorstep.

I convinced myself that if I took a step back, this

would all work out on its own. Besides, I wasn't quite sure what to do now that I'd finally admitted I did have feelings for Barry. But feeling something was as far as I was willing to take it, unless one of us left the company, and despite my pronouncement at the conference, I had no plans to do that.

The next morning I arrived early for work. As I entered my office, the telephone rang. I picked up the receiver and heard Barry's voice. He must have seen me pass by his office.

"Hi, can you come to my office, please?"

"Sure, Barry. I'll be there shortly." I knocked on the door and entered when signaled. I tried my level best to act normal, whatever that was, but my heart was pounding so loudly, I thought he might be able to hear it.

He made small talk. "How was your flight home?"

"Okay. How was yours?"

He looked terrible, as though he hadn't slept in weeks. Well, that made two of us. He motioned for me to sit, cleared his throat, and looked down at his desk as he spoke to me in a low voice.

"I can't begin to tell you how embarrassed I am about my actions. I don't know what came over me." He cleared his throat again. "I was being truthful when I asked you to stay, because you're already the best assistant I've ever had."

"Oh, really?" I said sarcastically. "If that's the case, why all the criticism?"

"I know. I'm just going through some turmoil right now, and I'm taking it out on you. But I am pleased with your performance. Obviously, I don't like it when you make errors."

"Look. You hired me based on my credentials, which were excellent. I'm not saying I'm perfect—not by a long shot—but it would be nice if you would offer up some kudos once in a while. You know how hard I work and the hours I put into this job."

He nodded his head in agreement, but his eyes remained focused on his desktop.

I lowered my head in order to make eye contact with him.

He looked up at me. "Cassie, I don't want you to leave, but if you're certain that's what you want, I'll understand. Just let me know your decision by close of business today."

My heart ached for the way he looked, and I could almost feel the embarrassment he was experiencing. I decided to give him a break.

"I've already made my decision. I'm staying."

"Thank you." He released a heavy breath. "I'm relieved to hear that."

I stood. "I'd better get back to my office. I have a ton of things to do."

I could tell he was feeling awkward about my being in his presence. I didn't feel too good about it either.

Victoria was at her desk when I walked by.

"Hey, how are you?" she asked.

I nodded in the affirmative. "I'm good."

"Something is wrong. I could feel it with Barry, and now I'm feeling it with you too."

"There you go again, letting that imagination of yours work overtime."

She shook her head, puzzled. "No. No, I'm not. You can cut the tension in here with a knife. Did you two have another argument?"

"No. I think it's still a carryover from the last one."

I smiled and waved as I walked down the hall to my office. The expression on Victoria's face told me she wasn't convinced.

Barry and I avoided each other for the remainder of the week. I was happy when Friday arrived. I was looking forward to cocktails with Meg, a trip to the spa for a massage, and just hanging out. I was glad Jason was out of town on business, so I wouldn't have to deal with him either. I just needed some down time. My mind needed a retreat.

At 5:00 I left the office and went home. Megan was sitting on the sofa, talking on the phone. I assumed it was Ralph, from the smile on her face. She pointed to the phone and mouthed his name. I nodded in acknowledgement and plopped down onto the sofa, kicked off my shoes, and put my feet up on the coffee table, waiting for her to finish.

"Okay," she said, "you have fun tonight. Yeah, Cassie and I are going out on the town." She looked over at me and smiled. "Or maybe not." She finished the call and gave me a curious look. "So, what's going on? How was your day?"

"Just dandy. How was yours?"

"Whoa. I don't like the sound of that. What's going on?"

"My life is a mess, and this weekend I'm taking a break from all the men in my life."

"Sounds serious. Want to talk now or later?"

"Let's get ready to go out. We can talk on the way."

On our way to the Slouching Turtle cocktail lounge, Megan said, "Okay, spill the beans. What's happened since last week?"

"Where do I begin?" I began to cry.

"Oh, Cass, don't cry. Talk to me—tell me what's been happening."

"My boss kissed me, and Jason wants an exclusive relationship," I said between sobs.

"Whoa!" she exclaimed. "When did all this happen?"

"And now Barry's avoiding me."

"Okay, take a deep breath, and fill in the missing pieces." She pulled tissues and a bottle of water from her bag. Here, take these and have a good cry. She gave me a sympathetic smile, making me cry even harder.

"Take a few swigs of water. Do you feel any better?"

I nodded. "Yeah, I think I've gotten it out of my system."

"Would you rather go home and have takeout tonight instead? Your eyes look like two puffballs."

"Do you mind?"

"Absolutely not. We can talk all night if you want. There's no one to bother us. Ralph is playing poker with his friends tonight, and Jason . . . where is he?"

"He's in Florida at a conference until Monday, I think."

"Good. Want Chinese food?" She patted my hand. "We can stop at Ling's China House on the way home."

"That would be nice. Thanks, Meg."

Chapter Sixteen

A ringing sound pierced my ears. When I realized it was the phone, I ignored it and rolled over, willing my body to recapture my comfortable state of slumber.

A few minutes later it rang again. I was relatively certain that whoever was on the other end was not going to give up until they got a hold of me. I lifted my eye mask, peeked at the clock on my dresser, and couldn't believe someone was calling at such an ungodly hour on a Saturday morning. I answered in a raspy voice.

"Hello?"

"Well, it's about time you answered!" my mother practically shouted into the phone.

"Mom? What's the matter?"

"Are you going to help your father or not? After all, you promised."

"Mother, what promise is this? It's six in the morning." I released a scornful groan. "You couldn't call me at a decent hour?"

"I knew it. It's just like you to renege. The catering job, remember?"

My mind foggy, I responded tersely. "What catering job?"

"I knew it! You're a real scatterbrain since you started working in New York, you know that?"

Desperately trying to shake loose the cobwebs in my head, I said, "Oh, wait a minute. Right, the catering job. When is it?"

"Today."

"Today?" I screeched, and I bolted from the bed. "You couldn't tell me the date when you left your message?"

"Well, you were supposed to call me back, and you didn't. If you had, I would have told you."

"Oh, that's just swell."

"Well, if you're not going to live up to your part of the bargain, *you* can call your father and tell him yourself. He'll just have to find someone else, but I don't know who he can get at this late hour."

I sighed. "No, I'm getting up. What time does Dad need me there?"

"Be here at eight—and make sure you bring the black-and-white uniform."

Frustrated, I asked, "Mother, is there a problem I don't know about? You've been awfully sharp with me over the last few months, and quite frankly, I really don't need any more grief in my life."

"Don't even get me started. Just be here in two hours." The line went dead.

"Let it go, Cassie," I told myself. "She's on one of her tirades, and it sounds like she's looking for someone to argue with."

I tried to think of something positive instead, but I wasn't having much luck, with the recent state of affairs.

I entered the shower and let cool water run down my body. My head ached from only three hours of sleep, my eyes were puffy, and the cool water wasn't doing the trick. I quickly exited the shower and dressed. I gulped down a glass of orange juice, grabbed a Twinkie from the cupboard, and headed out.

Mom was on the phone when I arrived. "Okay, that's good. Yes, she is. Did Michael give you directions to the job? Uh-huh. Okay. Yeah, that's great. Then you're all set." She quickly hung up the phone when I walked up to her.

"Hi, Mom." I leaned over and kissed her. "Who was that?" I asked.

"The bartender," she said coolly.

"Wow, this sounds like a pretty important party. How many people are attending, and how many of us are working?"

"There are eighty guests, so your father thinks five waitresses and one bartender ought to do it."

"Do I know this customer?"

"No, I don't think you've met her," she answered, then went about her business. "These people are on the society pages in the newspaper . . . you know, the muckety-mucks of Nutley."

Dad walked into the room, his arms spread apart, ready to give me the customary bear hug.

I walked right into his arms. "Dad, it's so nice to see you."

I adored the man and the ease with which we communicated with each. I knew he'd never judge me, no matter how off the wall my aspirations were. He was always supportive and loving.

"Hey, thanks for helping me out today, Cass. I really appreciate it."

"I know you do." I gave him an affectionate smile. "So where's the food? It smells so good in here."

"Already in the truck. You want to ride over with me?"

"Sure. Mom, are you coming with us?"

"No, I'm going to stay here in case your father needs anything. You'll be coming back here after the party, right?"

I shrugged. "I'm here on three hours' sleep, so I'm not sure. It depends on how tired I am. But I'll come over one night this week if you'd like some company."

Her face lit up like a Christmas tree. "Okay, why don't you and Megan come for dinner?"

"That would be terrific. I haven't had your cooking in weeks." *Uh-oh, dummy, wrong thing to say.*

She held a hand up like a stop sign. "Like I said

before, don't get me started." She rolled her eyes. "Well, you guys better get out of here. You don't want to keep the Dragon Lady waiting."

"Dragon Lady?" I recalled an earlier conversation Mom and I had had about this woman. "Oh, I remember your telling me about her." I scrunched up my face. "Hope she's nice today."

"I wouldn't count on it," Mom said.

Dad pulled up to the gates, pressed the intercom to announce his arrival, and they opened.

We drove ahead on a long lane leading up to the main house. I inhaled the strong scent of pine coming through the air vents.

"Mmm, I love the smell of pine. It makes me think of Christmas," I said.

"Yeah, me too," Dad replied.

The driveway was lined with pine trees on each side. High stone walls blocked the view of the private residence from the street, but it soon became visible to us. It was gorgeous.

"Wow!" I exclaimed. "Talk about lifestyles of the rich and famous."

"Yeah, isn't this place something? She's my best customer, but, boy, is she high maintenance. She complains a lot, and she's a demanding pain in the butt, but she never squabbles about the price. I hand her the bill, and she hands me the check. She always throws in extra cash for the wait staff too."

We stopped the van at the front entrance. I walked around to the back and opened the doors, while Dad walked up the steps to the door and rang the bell. A maid answered and let him in. A few minutes later Dad returned with help in tow. I pulled out a tray and turned to hand it to someone, and found myself face-to-face with Sammy Scarliotti. Startled, I jumped back.

"Hi, Cassie. It's nice to see you again."

Surprised, all I could do was nod. He took the tray and walked up the steps and into the house. I shot Dad a look, my lips pursed. "What is he doing here?"

He shrugged. "Bartending. But it wasn't my idea, Cass." He held up a hand. "I swear."

"Humph," I grumbled. "I have no doubt, Dad."

"Actually, though, if you'd let yourself get to know him, Sammy's really a nice guy. But you know me—I'm not pushing," he said reassuringly. "That has to be your decision. But I'm sure you'll be professional for the sake of the party, right?"

Before I could answer, Sammy was back and standing next to me, a big smile on his face. I glared at him as he grabbed my hand and planted a kiss on my cheek. I jerked my hand out of his and wiped his kiss off with my shoulder.

"I'm sorry. I didn't mean to get you wet."

I gave him a dirty look and pulled another tray from the rack.

"Here, let me get that for you," he said, taking the tray from my hands. "When can we get together again?"

I ignored his question, pretending I didn't hear him. I continued removing the trays and passed them out. He finally took the hint and walked into the house. When the van was empty, I entered the house with everyone else, and we began to set up tables and serving stations.

A momentary ripple of guilt overcame me for my behavior toward Sammy, but it quickly vanished when I thought about Mom's sneaky tactics. I probably should have been upset with Dad too, for not telling me that I'd be spending the afternoon with Sammy, but he doesn't have it easy, living with the domineering Lucy Pirelli.

We completed setting up just in time for the "dragon lady" to make her grand entrance. She sashayed down the spiral staircase, looking very elegant in a long red skirt and satin blouse. Her short dark hair was quite stylish, and I might have considered her pretty if not for the snooty look on her face. Having heard so many negative things about her, I half expected to see horns growing out of her head.

She approached Dad, and I overheard her ask to be introduced, to make sure we all understood just how important this party was to her and the children's benefit she was hosting.

"This is Mrs. Davis, everyone." He turned to face her. "Allow me to introduce my staff—Cassie, Julie, Sandra, Marge, Karen, and Sammy."

Intimidation welled in my stomach. She asked us to line up as she walked back and forth the way General Patton might have, inspecting his troops.

The minute she stopped in front of me, I knew this woman was going to be trouble. As she leered at me, I got the impression she already thought I was inept. In an instant her eyebrows arched, and her finger began wagging in my face as though I was a child.

"Cassie, make sure that blouse of yours is tucked in properly before my guests arrive. I don't want them thinking I have the Bad News Bears working for me tonight."

I turned and looked at Dad. He could tell I was getting upset by the expression on my face, and he walked over, grabbed my hand, and squeezed it.

"Absolutely, Mrs. Davis. Cassie was busy setting up. My staff is well trained. You don't need to worry."

"Okay, Michael, I'm taking you at your word." She spun on her heels and walked away.

"I'm sorry I didn't tuck my blouse in first before she came over here to meet us," I said apologetically, "but she came by so soon after we finished setting up, I didn't have a chance."

"It's okay. Don't worry." He squeezed my hand again. "She's just nervous. You know, she's a high-profile attorney, and word is that she's vying for a judgeship in the State Supreme Court."

He gave me a compassionate smile. "She'll be fine. Try to avoid her as much as you can, though. At every event she seems to single out one of the servers for criticism." His head tilted to one side. "I'm afraid it's you this time."

I shrugged. "Thanks for the warning. I'll be fine."

The witching hour arrived, and so did the guests. A harpist was playing a beautiful melody and trying to ignore Mrs. Davis as she flitted around making sure the hired hands knew what she expected of them.

I arranged hot hors d'oeuvres on a tray in the kitchen and headed out to the ballroom-sized dining room to begin serving the guests. I glanced over at the bar and noticed Sammy handing a tray of filled Champagne glasses to one of the other servers. He glanced my way, and I pretended not to notice.

My parents might have a soft spot for the guy, but as far as I was concerned, the jury was still out on him. After all, he'd tried to cop a cheap feel in my parents' home.

The event was progressing rather nicely. But with only three hours' sleep under my belt, the strain of deprivation began to take hold, and I was eager for the occasion to end.

I took a quick break and watched the guests enjoying themselves.

Sammy left the bar and walked over to me. "Cassie, may I talk to you for a minute?"

"Yeah. What do you want?"

"Why don't you like me? What did I ever do to you?"

"Excuse me? What did you do to me? I think you know perfectly well what you did."

"I do?" He ran his fingers through his hair as he pondered. "Oh, wait. Are you referring to your outburst when we were sitting in the living room at your parents' house, and you shouted at me and called me Bucko? I think that's what you called me. After your mother walked in and escorted us into the dining room for dinner, you never brought the subject up again, so I figured whatever it was couldn't have been that important. Would you care to tell me what that was all about, so we can move forward?"

"I can't believe you're pretending not to know what that was all about." I shot him an angry look. "I'm not accustomed to having men try to sneak a feel, especially in my parents' home."

He got a look of shock on his face. "Are you out of your mind? What made you think I was doing that?"

"Sure, go ahead and pretend," I said sarcastically. "Look, my break is over, and I have to get back to work." I walked away from him and returned to retrieve a tray filled with canapés.

He headed back toward the bar, then suddenly changed his mind and walked after me. He grabbed my elbow and tried to slow me down. With tray in hand, I kept walking swiftly to the center of the room to continue serving more guests.

In my haste to get away, I tripped and collided with someone, sending the tray I carried sailing through the air like a Frisbee. Screaming broke out as several guests quickly moved out of the way.

I felt like I was watching a movie in slow motion as I saw my tray slam into the Champagne tray one of the other waitresses carried, causing it to topple. I could hear my heart beating in my ears. Panic set in when I caught a glimpse of the damage.

Then I noticed a lady on the floor, apparently the result of my crashing into her. She sat up, confused, trying to collect her bearings. She rubbed liquid from her eyes and wiped her nose, never realizing she was making a fashion statement with her bald head exposed for all to see. I became paralyzed when I realized it was Mrs. Davis, the Dragon Lady.

Someone shouted. "There's a rat on the floor!" The group panicked, running out to the terrace as if someone yelled *"Fire!"*

Unfortunately for me, that so-called "rat" was the fallen wig. I reached over and snatched it off the floor. It was dripping with Champagne and Brie, but if I was going to save the hostess from additional embarrassment, I had no choice but to quickly cover her head and pray the guests were preoccupied with the mess surrounding us. My sticky fingers stuck to the strands of hair while I struggled to arrange the hairpiece properly. Since time was of the essence, I fumbled until the wig was securely sitting on her head—or so I thought. Unfortunately, with my inability to determine which end was up, the wig wound up cockeyed.

I heard laughter from behind me. Apparently some of the guests had witnessed the fiasco. Mrs. Davis was intensely humiliated and glared at me through black raccoon eyes, while drops of Champagne ran down her forehead. Before I knew it, a larger crowd of guests gathered around to watch the two of us sitting in a pool of shattered glass, alcohol, and Brie en croute. Mrs. Davis' head swung back and forth so quickly as she tried to absorb what was happening that some of the Brie dislodged itself from the wig and bounced off her nose.

When she sensed her wig was improperly resting on her head, she reached up and tried to fix it. I heard her mumble and look at me with contempt.

"I'm going to kill you, Cassie. You have totally ruined my party, and I'll never forgive your boss for bringing you to my home."

Dad and Sammy ran over as quickly as their legs could carry them and made their way through the crowd to help the damsels in distress. When Dad saw the two of us on the floor in a pool of liquid, the look on his face said it all. He reached for Mrs. Davis' hand to help her stand, while Sammy reached down and helped me. I was upset with Sammy for placing me in this predicament. After all, it was his fault this had happened in the first place.

I thought Mrs. Davis was literally going to explode. She looked at me with fire in her eyes, and she made a quick dash down a hallway, screaming, "Get that incompetent moron out of my house!"

Dad put an arm around me. "Cassie. Are you okay?"

I nodded. "A bruised ego perhaps, but I'm physically okay. I am so sorry. I tripped right into her."

Fortunately, the other workers managed to escort the guests to the outdoor patio to continue the festivities, giving us time to clean up the mess. As I began to move,

I noticed some soreness in my elbow and left thigh. I guess I hadn't realized how hard I'd hit the floor. I rubbed my elbow and winced from the pain. "Um, on second thought, maybe I'm not okay."

"Where does it hurt?"

"Don't worry, Dad. I'll be fine."

"You took quite a spill," Sammy said sadly.

I shot him an angry look. He took the hint and headed back to the bar.

Dad looked on, his brow furrowed in a frown. "What happened here?"

"I . . . um . . . accidentally slipped on something and fell. I tried to break my fall and grabbed the first thing I could. That 'thing' turned out to be Mrs. Davis—and her wig," I said. "Man, does it get any worse than this? The one person I was trying to avoid, and she had to be in the same spot I was. I am so sorry, Dad. I ruined your catering job."

He looked at me with consternation. "Hey, what are you going to do? It was an accident." He shrugged. "I'll talk to Mrs. Davis when she returns. She'll be fine."

"I'll apologize to her, Dad."

"No," he said emphatically. "Let me handle this."

A knot formed in my stomach. The last thing I wanted was to hurt Dad's business, but somehow I always managed to screw up something. Maybe Mom was right about me.

"Go to the bathroom and get cleaned up," Dad said gently.

Sammy stared at me from across the room. I turned my head in the opposite direction—his was the last face I wanted to see. None of this would have happened if he'd just left me alone.

I returned from the bathroom and began to help the others clean up the mess I'd made.

Later, when the party was over, Mrs. Davis was nowhere in sight. I walked over to Dad, who was helping the staff clean up. He looked up when he heard my footsteps.

"Did you speak to Mrs. Davis?"

"Not yet, sweetie. Please stop worrying. It will be okay."

I nodded with reluctance, hoping things really would be okay. I pitched in with the cleanup. After everything was packed, I carried the chafing dishes and utensils out to the van, placed everything back on the racks, and secured them with straps.

Sammy carried the last few things and handed them to me. He looked at me. "Are you okay, Cassie?"

"Don't speak to me. Just leave me alone, will you?"

He stood looking at me with a hurt expression on his face.

"What is it that you don't understand about 'leave me alone'?"

"Okay, Cassie, if that's the way you want it. But I just don't understand what it is I did to warrant your dislike for me."

"You're my mother's choice—don't you get it?"

"Is that what this is about?" He looked at me with disbelief. "You're kidding, right?"

"No, I'm afraid not."

He threw his arms into the air. "Fine, if that's the way you really want it. But you have no idea what you're missing."

"Oh, gag me."

He turned and headed to his own vehicle.

I waited in the van for Dad, who was undoubtedly trying to smooth things over with Mrs. Davis. A short time later he opened the door, slid behind the steering wheel, and drove out the driveway. I watched his profile as he clenched his jaw. I felt terrible.

"Dad? How did it go with Mrs. Davis?"

"Okay, I guess."

"What did she say? Is she mad at you?"

He chuckled. "Eh, she'll get over it."

"Do you think she'll ask you to cater again?"

"Of course she will. She pulls this kind of stuff all the time. We're talking about a flighty woman here. The only thing I can say is that she knows that your Mom and I make the best food in town. Don't you worry about anything." He snickered. "She did give me one condition, though."

"Yeah, I know. She wants you to fire me."

He nodded. "Yep, that pretty much sums it up." He reached over and grabbed my hand. "I'll use my best schmoozing techniques the next time she's in the shop."

Guilt-ridden, I leaned my head back and shut my

eyes. What was happening to me? First it was the issue with Jason, then Barry, and now this. I was feeling utterly dejected. I'd ruined Dad's catering job with one of his most valued customers, and I hadn't been very nice to Sammy, who really hadn't done anything wrong.

We pulled into the parking lot behind my parents' building. I got out on my side of the van and walked over to Dad, giving him a tight hug. "I'm really sorry, Dad."

"I know, Cass. Go home and get some rest. It will all work out." He reached into his pocket and pulled out a wad of bills and began counting them out.

"Oh, Dad, don't you even think about it." I pushed his hand back. "Thank you anyway, but I really don't want any money."

"Don't do that. You worked hard today." He shoved the money into my pocket.

"I really don't want it, but I know I'm not going to win this argument. Besides, I've caused enough problems for one day. I'm going to leave. I can't face Mom right now."

"I understand. Get home safely."

When I got home, I unlocked the door and called out to Megan.

"In here!" she shouted.

I entered the living room, where Megan and Ralph sat. They both stared at me, clearly curious. "What happened to you? You look like something the cat dragged in," Meg said.

"If only it was that simple."

Ralph noticed the look of desperation on my face. "You know what? I think you two need some time for girl talk."

"You're a smart guy, Ralph," I said gratefully. "Thanks."

He leaned over and kissed Megan on the cheek. "I'll call you later." On his way past me, he stopped to pinch my cheek. "Whatever it is, it'll be all right."

"Thanks. I needed that."

"I have to take a shower first," I said, "so you can stay a little longer."

I walked into the bedroom and undressed, removing my champagne-marinated clothing, and stepped into a hot, steamy shower. I lathered my hair with soap to remove the stickiness. Thoughts of the accident made me shudder, especially when I pictured the disappointed look on Dad's face. Knowing I'd caused the mishap while trying to get away from Sammy made me feel twice as bad. I can be such a jerk sometimes.

I exited the shower and toweled myself off. I slipped into my bathrobe, wrapped a towel around my wet hair, and walked back out into the living room. Ralph had already left. Megan sat with an opened box of Belgian chocolates. She shoved the box at me. "Here. Have some chocolate."

I shuddered and shook my head vigorously. "Please, get that stuff away from me."

Megan's eyes went wide with surprise. "What? Are we on the wagon?"

"Yeah. Maybe forever."

"Uh-oh. This is bad." She patted the sofa. "Sit and tell me about it."

Tears welled up in my eyes. "My life is such a mess. I really don't know what I'm doing anymore."

Megan gave me a sympathetic look. "What? Talk to me."

"This has been a day from hell." I sighed. "Mom called at the crack of dawn to tell me this was the day for the catering job. Why couldn't she have mentioned the date on the last message?"

"Okay, Cass, deep breath."

"Well, now you have a pretty good idea of how my day started off on the wrong foot. To make matters worse, when I arrived at the catering sight, who do you think the bartender was?"

Her brow furrowed. "Who?"

"Sammy Scarliotti," I said sharply.

"Oh, Cass, I'm so sorry. So tell me what happened."

"Where do I begin?" I rubbed my temples with my fingertips. "I have such a headache."

Megan got up, found a bottle of aspirin, dropped two pills into the palm of my hand, and handed me a glass of water.

"Okay, two more deep breaths."

"I suppose I should start with the last date I had with Jason."

I continued to fill her in on all the details of my disastrous life. We talked until I could no longer keep my eyes open.

"Thanks so much for listening." I yawned. "I need to get to bed. I'm too pooped to pop." I gave her a hug. "Thanks again, my friend."

"Good night. When your head is clearer, you'll come to a decision that's right for you."

"Yeah, I guess I will. I only wish I knew what that was."

Chapter Seventeen

I arrived at the office, my stomach in knots, knowing I had to face Barry's cold shoulder and Jason's looks of longing.

Victoria sat behind her desk. When she saw me, she grinned from ear to ear. "Boy, Cassie, you are one lucky lady."

"I am? Would you care to elaborate on that?"

"You, my friend, had yet another floral delivery. Red roses, to be precise. Do you know what red roses symbolize?"

"I'm sure you're going to tell me."

"It's love," she said enthusiastically. "So who's the lucky guy?"

My heart skipped a beat as I wondered. "I have no idea," I said honestly.

She pointed toward Barry's closed door and whispered, "Maybe they're from him again."

"Why would he be sending me flowers?" *Oh, please tell me she doesn't know about the kiss.*

"Are you still going to tell me you didn't see him staring at you the whole night during the party? And then you went to Dallas together . . ."

"Oh, stop. He's still angry with me over my carelessness on that other presentation. Haven't you noticed that we've hardly spoken? Have you seen us together? Out to lunch?"

"First of all, that presentation is ancient history. The fact that I haven't seen him speaking to you might not have anything to do with the presentation fiasco—but it might have to do with his avoiding you for some other reason," she said coyly.

I pursed my lips. "Victoria, just stop. You're way over the top on this one."

I headed toward my office but stopped when I realized she was behind me. I turned around to face her and chuckled. "Victoria, where are you going?"

"Hey, I want to know who sent the flowers. The suspense is killing me, and since I've been waiting patiently for you to arrive, I figured I'm entitled to know."

Panic set in. My mind began to race, wondering how I was going to get her to back off without offending her. What if it *was* Barry?

"Okay, I'll tell you what. You go back to your office, and I'll let you know who they're from."

"Aha! I thought so. You do know who sent them, and you just don't want me to know."

"That's so not true. They're probably from my dad . . . I don't know. I've had one hell of a weekend, so please be nice to me."

"Hey, I thought we were friends. I've shared lots of things with you that I don't want other people to know."

I couldn't argue with that. We had shared a lot—but she didn't know that Barry had kissed me—at least I was hoping she didn't—or that Jason had said he was falling in love with me. We reached my office and walked in. The sweet fragrance of roses engulfed us. I gasped when I looked at the arrangement. There had to be three dozen roses in a crystal vase with a huge red velvet bow. My heart began to beat faster.

"See what I mean, lucky woman?" Victoria exclaimed. "The guy who sent these must really mean it. Hurry, read the card."

The flowers were gorgeous. I was quite impressed myself. I pulled the envelope off the stick and opened the card.

Anger set in when I read the name on the gift card.

Victoria squealed, "Tell me!"

I frowned and handed her the vase. "Here, they're yours."

"Are you out of your mind? I'm not taking these flowers. Whoever sent them is madly in love with you," she said, holding a hand up to stop me. "So who is it?" she asked impatiently.

"Sammy."

"Sammy?" she asked.

"You know, the guy my mother has been trying to fix me up with. I don't want any part of these flowers—or Sammy, for that matter. Now please get them out of my office."

"You really have a major dislike for this guy. What is it that he did to you?"

"He's my mother's choice."

"So what. Is he a nice guy?"

"Yeah, he's okay."

"And you don't like him why?"

"He's my mother's choice," I repeated.

"So what does that have to do with anything? And what does he say on the card?"

"You wouldn't understand. And he just signed his name."

"I think you're fibbing, but okay. I'll let you off the hook." She headed for the door without the roses.

I called, "Take the roses, or I'll call the florist and have them returned to the sender."

"You're unbelievable." She walked over to the credenza, lifted them up, and turned, heading toward the door.

I sat back in my chair, staring into space, the card still in my hand. I glanced at it again and read his message. *I'm so sorry for the way things have turned out so far. I really want to get to know you. Can't we please work this out? Love, Sammy.*

"Not a chance," I said aloud. The phone rang, and I reached for the receiver.

"Good morning, this is Cassie Pirelli."

"Hi, Cass."

"Leave me alone, Sammy."

"Hey, you finally recognized my voice. Perhaps there's hope for us after all."

"Don't flatter yourself."

He sighed. "Did you receive the flowers I sent?"

"I did—and I've given them to the secretary. What is it about *no* that you don't understand?"

"Cassie, why do you make this such a challenge?"

"Listen, Bucko, there is no challenge here. I'm not interested—so you can tell my mother to back off too. Do you get it now?"

"I think you're making a big mistake. I can offer you something you've only dreamed about."

"Yeah, but I'm not dreaming about it with you—so back off." I slammed the receiver back into its cradle. A few minutes later the phone rang again.

I picked up the receiver and began to say my name, when the caller interrupted me.

"I'm not giving up on you, Cassie. You can say all the mean things you want, but in the end, you're going to be mine." He clicked the receiver in my ear.

"Yeah, in *your* dreams, buddy!" I shouted.

I buzzed Victoria on the intercom. "Please hold all my calls. I have a lot of work to do, and I don't want to be interrupted."

"You've got it. What should I tell the boss if he wants to speak to you?"

"I don't think we need to worry about that one, but sure, if he does, just buzz me."

"Okay. One more thing. Want to have lunch today?"

"I can't today. Maybe tomorrow, though." I clicked the intercom off. First solution for the day. Avoid everyone. I know, not very mature on my part, but I've created enough havoc around here lately.

At 5:30 the buzz of the intercom jolted me from my concentration. Victoria wanted to tell me she was leaving for the day.

"Thank you for understanding my need for silence today, Victoria. You have a good evening."

"You're welcome. Maybe tomorrow will be better for you."

"I think it will. Good night."

I continued to work diligently on the Benson file. Hours later, fatigued, I glanced at the clock and noticed it was 9:00 P.M. I stood and stretched. I'd been sitting all day, and I was stiff. A heavy, grumbling noise came from my stomach, signaling that the peanuts I'd been munching on all day hadn't been enough sustenance.

I swiftly cleared my desk, packed my briefcase, and walked past Victoria's station, when I noticed Jason leaning over it, writing a note. He looked up when he heard my footsteps.

"Hey, I wondered when you'd come up for air. I've been trying to reach you all day."

"Hi, Jase. Yeah, I had a pile of work that I needed to prepare for a meeting. Sorry I missed you. Was there something you wanted?"

He chuckled. "Only to tell you that I missed you." He moved closer, engulfing me in his arms, and gave me a long, passionate kiss. "It's good to see you."

I shifted with unease and stepped back. "Ah, Jason. We need to talk."

He grinned like the Cheshire Cat. He took the briefcase from my grip and extended his arm for me to latch on to. "That's good, because we have a nine-thirty dinner reservation at Sirocco's. I know you haven't eaten all day because I checked with Victoria."

"All right. I really do need to speak to you."

"Great. That works for me. We have a corner table, so you can talk to your heart's content."

We drove in silence. Mine was from exhaustion and a cluttered mind. His—well, I don't know what his was from, but I was certain I would hear something soon. We walked into the restaurant. The hostess apparently knew Jason, since she called him Mr. Reed and escorted us to our table.

In a boyish, playful voice, he said, "Okay, the floor is yours. Speak to me."

I cleared my throat. I smiled and began. "I wanted to speak to you about your phone call."

His spirits seemed to soar with delight.

Uh-oh. I need to find another way of approaching this. "I hope you'll understand what I'm about to say."

His demeanor became more serious. "Okay, go ahead."

"When I took this job at Merrill, it was with the sole intent of moving up the corporate ladder. While I enjoy being with you and the friendship we've developed, I'm just not ready to focus on a relationship."

He reached across the table and grabbed my hand. A confident grin crossed his face. "Cassie Pirelli, from the first day I met you, it didn't take me long to figure out how goal-oriented you are—I accept that. My career goals are just as important to me. I personally think you can have both, but I'll accept your decision."

"Thank you for making this easy." I was feeling pleased with myself, basically because I'd finally gotten my point across, and I hadn't insulted him.

"However, what you don't know about me is that I don't give up easily—so I'm willing to wait as long as it takes to win your heart."

So much for getting my point across.

"Um, Jason, I guess what I'm trying to say is that I'm just not sure of my feelings for you. I don't want to lead you on in any way, then have you disappointed when I don't respond."

"Right. I know," he said as he nodded. "I understand completely." A sheepish grin exposed his perfect white teeth. "But you have no idea what I'm capable of once I pull out all the stops. I'm willing to do whatever it takes to sweep you off your feet."

I took a swig of Pellegrino, realizing I'd accomplished

absolutely nothing with my little speech. *Maybe there's another way of saying this.* But I was mentally exhausted from the events of the past few weeks, and I was ready to run away and change my name and not tell anyone where I was going.

He changed the subject. "So, what did you do yesterday?"

"I had the day from hell."

"What happened?"

"I helped my father cater a party for one of his customers."

"Really? I didn't know your father was a caterer."

"He actually owns an Italian deli in Nutley and also does catering. I'd promised him I would help with a party."

"Wasn't it fun?"

I giggled. "Hardly! The hostess took an instant dislike to me. I have no idea why, but she picked on me all day. After that, things went downhill faster than a roller coaster."

"I'm sorry to hear that." He grinned, "See, you should have come to Florida with me."

I released a heavy sigh. "Oh, Jason, what am I going to do with you? I really didn't expect you to fall in love with me. I just thought we were friends."

His expression changed. "Do you have something against falling in love?"

"No, it's just that I don't think of you in a romantic

way. You're my buddy . . . like the big brother I never had, and I don't want to ruin that."

"I thought we discussed this friendship thing before. Being friends is part of the package in romance, isn't it?"

"Yes, I suppose it is, but—"

He interrupted. "Okay, let's just continue in the same vein, and we'll cross that bridge when we come to it. Fair enough?"

"Fair enough."

Chapter Eighteen

I sat in my office drinking coffee, when I heard the intercom buzz. I pushed the button. "Good morning, Barry."

"Good morning, Cassie. Can you come into my office?"

"Sure, when? Right now?"

"Yes, please."

"I'm on my way." I grabbed my notebook and headed down the hall. When I reached his office, I knocked on the door and entered. Much to my surprise, there was another good-looking man sitting in his office. Barry looked up with a smile and gestured to his guest. "Cassie, I'd like you to meet Michael Ramsey. Michael, meet Cassie Pirelli."

I nodded and extended my hand. "How do you do, Michael? Nice to meet you."

Barry continued. "Cassie, Michael has just accepted a position here at Merrill, and he'll be writing my presentations."

A knot tightened in my throat. Confused, I mumbled a faint, "Oh, okay. When does he begin?"

"Today. Victoria is out sick, so I was wondering if you wouldn't mind taking him around to meet everyone."

"Sure, Barry."

"Oh, and let him use the vacant office next to yours."

I felt my body tighten. My legs began to wobble like a bowlful of jelly. I couldn't believe my ears, wondering what was going on and why Barry hadn't spoken to me first before he'd sprung this surprise on me.

"After I get Michael settled," I said, "I'd like to spend some time with you. I have something I'd like to discuss. Preferably early afternoon."

He avoided eye contact with me and answered, "Okay, how about one-thirty?"

"That would be fine." I turned to Michael and smiled. "Well, are you ready to meet the rest of the staff?"

He answered in an excited voice, "Absolutely! I've waited a long time to get into this company. I'm ready for anything."

I tried to calm myself and not jump to any conclusions about Michael's taking over part of my duties. I was anxious about my meeting with Barry, but that would have to wait until later. When the tour concluded, I walked Michael to his office, and I left him alone to savor his moment of joy.

I walked into my office and closed the door behind me. I sat for a while wondering what Barry had up his sleeve. Was I being fired? I could feel a slow burn building inside me and took a deep breath, trying to relax. At one-thirty Barry called me to his office again.

"What's going on here, Barry? Why did you hire Michael to take over part of my duties?"

He looked up at me. "Slow down, Cassie. He's not taking over your job, just one aspect of it. I just think it would be better for him to write my presentations. You have an overabundance of work with the event-planning end of it and dealing with customer issues, so I think having Michael here will give you more time to do those things."

"Let me get this straight," I snapped. "You're saying this is a gift to me? Is that right?"

"Well, yes." He scratched his head. "Yes, I think that's exactly the way you should look at it."

"Fine, if that's the way you want it." I stood and began walking out in a huff. My anger got the best of me, and I stopped to look at him. "Barry, is this about Dallas? Is that it?"

A sad look crossed his face. "Well, I guess you could say that—indirectly, that is. It's not because I kissed you, though. It's because I'm having a hard time dealing with it."

"*You* can't deal with it?"

"I broke my own rules by falling for you. I swore I'd remain single . . . until you came along, and I was willing to throw caution to the wind and break more rules—company rules."

I stood with my mouth open in surprise as he continued.

"You gave me back something I haven't felt in a very long time. I don't like the idea of hiring someone to replace you on my trips, but that's the way it has to be."

He began to pace. His hand ruffled his hair. "I misread our interactions. I thought you felt the same way about me. I would have risked everything to see you secretly, even though I know it's against company policy—and even though I've fired employees for doing that very thing." He shook his head. "Why did you have to be so damn cute?"

I stood in silence, trying to take in what my ears were hearing. I did care for him, but telling him now would only sound like I wanted to get back into his good graces.

"I . . . I don't know what to say to you."

He smirked. "You don't have to say anything. Are we finished here?"

"Yes." I turned to leave. "I'm very sorry for everything." I walked to my office and gathered my belongings. I needed to get out of there. I couldn't concentrate on anything anyway.

I made some excuse to Victoria, hailed a cab, and headed for home, wondering what I was going to do and how I could work this out. I walked into the apartment and sat in the living room, stunned. "What have I done? I just let the man of my dreams slip right through my fingers—all because of my ambition?"

I couldn't call Megan to console me. She was on vacation with a group of office friends, and I didn't want to upset her. I'd already done more than enough to upset people.

I sat for what seemed like hours trying to mull over everything and what my course of action should be.

I walked into the bedroom, flopped onto my bed, and closed my eyes to shut out reality. I fell asleep until morning.

The phone rang, and I slowly moved to answer it.

"Hi, Cassie," Mom said. "I'm glad I caught you."

Oh, please let this be over soon.

"Hi."

"What's wrong? Are you okay?"

"No, I really don't feel well." I checked the clock and was surprised it was so late.

"What's the matter? Did you catch a bug?"

"No, I must have eaten something to upset my stomach."

"Well, that doesn't surprise me a bit. How long was whatever you ate sitting in the refrigerator? Did it have fuzzy things growing on it? You and Megan are 'career women.' " She let out a cynical chuckle. "No time for being domestic. Let me come over and make some pastina and chicken broth for you."

"No. That's okay. Really. That's very nice of you, but I'll be fine as soon as I take a shower. I didn't realize it

was so late, so I'd better run and get into the shower before my boss has a fit."

"Oh, no, you don't," she said with authority. "You're
not going into work with the way you sound. Get back
into bed. I'm coming over."

I was in no mood to argue, so I agreed to let her do
her thing. What I really wanted was to be able to con-
fide in her, but knew I couldn't, because she wouldn't
understand.

I pressed the disconnect button, then dialed the office
to leave a message for Victoria, informing her I was
taking a sick day.

I crawled back under the covers and must have
fallen back to sleep. I was awakened by Mom, who
called out to me.

"Cassie, I'm here." I got out of bed and walked into
the living room to greet her. She was carrying an arm-
ful of bags.

"How'd you get in?"

"I asked the super to let me in. I did ring the bell, but
I guess you didn't hear it."

"Oh." I actually was glad she'd come. It made me
feel like a child again.

"Okay, you rest. I'll be in the kitchen."

"Thanks, Mom," I said.

I must have dozed off again and didn't wake until she
walked in carrying a tray with a bowl of her cure-all soup.

"How do you feel?" she said, adjusting the pillows
behind my back. "I brought you some soup." The aroma

from the bowl brought back memories of the many tender moments Mom and I had shared while I was growing up, the way she pampered me when I was sick. I wondered what had happened to them. Where they'd gone and why.

"Are you feeling any better?" she said, easing herself down on the edge of my bed.

"I'm sure I will as soon as I eat this soup." I devoured the bowl's contents as if I hadn't eaten in weeks.

"You were pretty hungry. Want some more?"

I touched her arm, and my eyes welled up with tears. "Mom, thanks for being here."

A look of empathy crossed her chubby face. "I'm happy to be here." She reached for my hand and held it tightly, rubbing it between her two hands. "What's wrong, honey? You don't have the flu. Talk to me, Cass."

I started bawling like a twelve-year-old. Mom hugged me tighter. Then she released me from the hug and looked me in the eye.

"Hey, nothing can be that bad. Tell me what the problem is, and maybe we can figure out how to fix it."

Knowing I had her support made me happy. I smiled affectionately at her. "Your daughter is a jerk. Do you know that?"

"We all make mistakes. Now, what's yours?" She handed me a tissue to blow my nose.

"I've fallen for my boss."

"So you do like men after all," she teased. "Judging from the look on your face, I guess falling for your boss is a bad thing?"

"Wait, there's more." I can't ever remember a time that my mother actually sat quietly and listened to my every word without interrupting.

When I finished, she smiled and grabbed my hand. "Okay, Cass, we can fix this. I have a plan." Mom filled me in on her grand scheme of how to handle the situation.

"Do you really think that will work?"

"Hey, it got your father's attention."

"Why, Mother, I had no idea you were so devious," I lied with a chuckle. "Gee, I'm learning all sorts of new things about you today."

She smiled. "You're feeling a little better, aren't you?"

I nodded and reached for her hand. "Thanks for listening."

My eyes welled with tears again. For years I'd yearned for her to show me the tenderness she displayed in those few minutes—a side of her I hadn't seen since I was a child.

"Mom, I love you. You do know that, don't you?"

"Wow! My cup runneth over today. I haven't heard you say that in a long time." She reached to hug me. "I'm so glad I called you when I did. I wouldn't have missed hearing those words for all the tea in China."

She held me at arm's length and stared into my eyes with a contented smile on her face. "By the way, if it's meant for you to be with this man, it will work. Just give it your best shot."

"Well, I think I should wait a while before I do it. I

need some time to think—I've already made too many mistakes. I sure don't need any more."

"You'll know when the time is right." She looked at the clock on the bureau. "Oh, Cass, if you're sure you're okay, I need to get home and cook dinner for your father," she said apologetically. "Hey, why don't you come home with me? You can spend the night."

"Well, I'd love to come for dinner, but I'd rather not spend the night. I have to get to the office tomorrow, and all my things are here. I'm really not in any mood to pack a bag." I smiled faintly. "With the state I'm in, I'd probably forget to pack something and wind up looking like a dork. I want to dazzle the man, not turn him off. You understand, don't you?"

She hugged me. "Of course I do. Okay, let me call Dad and tell him we're on our way. You go wash your face and comb your hair. You're an absolute mess," she teased.

We arrived at the apartment. Dad was delighted to see us.

The nonstop chatter and laughter around the table was just the warmth I needed. Being with my family felt as comfortable an old pair of shoes. The contented smile on Mom's face was priceless, causing a deluge of emotions to flood through my mind. I wondered if the many stunts she'd pulled over the past few years was simply her way of getting my attention.

I needed to stop adding more crap to the pile. I'd had more than my share of trauma over the past several weeks—enough to last me a lifetime. I promised myself that, moving forward, I would make an honest effort to avoid as many confrontations with Mom as possible and give *her* the emotional support *she* needed. I knew we weren't always going to agree with each other, but I'd give it my best shot.

"Well, hello, Cass," Victoria said as I passed her office. "Are you feeling better?"

"Oh, much better, thanks. I'm sure I have tons of work waiting for me, so I'll catch up with you later."

She raised a hand in agreement and continued to type.

My desk had a stack of files waiting for me. Leafing through the pile, I wondered where Barry and Michael were, since I hadn't seen them. I buzzed Victoria on the intercom.

"You rang, my dear?"

"Hey, where is Barry today? I must have misplaced his calendar, and you know what that means, don't you?"

"Yeah, I'll make you another copy. But to answer your question, he's in New Orleans with Michael."

"Hmm, for some reason I thought that conference was next week," I lied, pretending I knew about it. "Did Michael write Barry's presentation?"

"Yes." She hesitated briefly. "Is there something I should know about here? I'm getting the distinct impression that this new guy is taking over your job. Are you leaving?"

I felt an ache of emptiness in the pit of my stomach. I faked a giggle. "I hope not."

"So why did Barry hire him?"

"Well, we've been getting extremely busy, and Michael is here to help with the workload. It'll be fine—not to worry," I responded halfheartedly. "Okay, thanks. I need to wade through this pile on my desk. Want to have lunch today?"

"I thought you'd never ask. We haven't had lunch together in ages. That would be great."

"Good, Vic. I'll see you at the regular time, then? Oh, and please hold my calls today. Judging from this pile on my desk, I may not surface until spring."

"Sure. See you later." We disconnected, and I returned to my work.

Barry and Michael returned from New Orleans by midweek. Michael indeed seemed to be taking over my job, and I didn't like it one bit.

Between Michael's taking over my role, and Barry's cold shoulder, I was developing an attitude. "Humph, I'll bet Michael isn't as creative as I am." I was so annoyed at both of them that I pounded a fist on my desk. I was jealous, and I knew it. Poor Michael hadn't done anything to me, and here I was thinking negative things about him.

My thoughts turned to all the men in my life. While I knew most women would have given their eyeteeth for that kind of luck, the only man I was interested in was Barry.

It was getting late, and I was tired. I began to think about how much I missed seeing Barry. I left my office and walked over to his. His office was dark, so I decided to call him at home. I dialed his number.

"Hello?"

"Hi, Barry." I nervously tapped my foot. My stomach was tied into knots.

"Hi. What can I do for you, Cassie?" he said in an aloof sort of way.

"Are you free for lunch tomorrow?"

"Ah . . . actually, I'm not. What's wrong?"

I heard a woman's voice in the background.

"Oh, nothing is wrong. I haven't seen you in a while, and I wondered how you were doing. Um, and I'd like to chat with you about something."

"Can we discuss this now, over the phone? I'm free at the moment—well, not really free, but this is as good a time as any."

I knew I deserved the deep freeze I was getting, but I couldn't help but feel sorry for myself. Hearing the woman's voice wasn't helping either. Disappointed, I said, "Well, I guess it can wait for another time. I'm pretty busy myself. Thanks anyway."

I returned the receiver to the cradle and immediately went into sulk mode. I tried to focus on my work but wasn't having much luck. I threw the material I was working on back into the file and left for home.

I returned to an empty apartment. Megan had returned from vacation but was out with Ralph somewhere. I plopped down onto the sofa and decided I was due for a good cry in the privacy of my own home and allowed the floodgates to open.

At nine in the evening my stomach began to rumble. I checked the cupboards for anything that resembled food, but old Mother Hubbard's cupboards were stark—no Twinkies, no cereal, nada. Neither Megan nor I had been grocery shopping in a while, so I decided to hit a local pub instead.

"Besides," I said, "the walk might help clear my head."

I entered The Pub just as the band was returning from a break, and I sat at a table, waiting for the waitress to approach. She walked over with pad in hand, and I ordered comfort food. Yep, I was going to have a freakin' food fest, and I didn't care if it was listed under the category of emotional eating.

A grin of amusement formed on the waitress's face as I ordered a burger, onion rings, mozzarella sticks, fried calamari, and a shake.

"And I also want your famous sundae. Make sure you add tons of chocolate fudge and caramel sauce. And—oh, yeah—don't forget lots of whipped cream and nuts."

Yep, I was having chocolate—the fast was over.

She cracked her gum. "Just broke up with the boyfriend, huh?" She patted my hand.

"How do you know—?" I never finished, because she headed toward the kitchen.

While I waited for my food, I started thinking about

my mantra of never giving up on something I really wanted. So why was this any different? I've always been a levelheaded woman. Where had that Cassie gone? I didn't understand what had happened to reduce me to this state of depression.

And then it was as if the light went on, and I realized I was having a difficult time because I was afraid of Barry's rejection. Sure, he'd told me he cared, but I hadn't said anything in return. I'd missed my window of opportunity, and now I was concerned I'd lost it forever.

I decided to forget the feast and get home to develop Mom's plan of action. I grabbed my purse and headed for the door.

The waitress ran after me. "Hey, where are you going? Your food is almost ready."

"Oh, I'm sorry," I lied. "I just got a call from my mother, and—"

She gave me a suspicious nod. "Yeah, right, and she's not feeling well. I'll be right back with your food. Don't you dare stiff me and leave without paying."

I stood impatiently tapping my fingers on the bar, eager to leave the noise and crowd behind. I paid the bill, exited the bar, and walked—well, actually, ran—home.

I entered my apartment and walked in on Megan and Ralph, who seemed to be having a serious conversation. I tried to tiptoe to my bedroom before they looked up, but my footsteps alerted them they weren't alone.

"Hey, Cass, where ya been?"

"I went to The Pub for a burger. I thought maybe

some of the gang would be there, but it seems there's a different crowd on Wednesdays."

Ralph frowned and looked at Megan. "Uh-oh. I see another girls' night coming on."

Megan looked at me quizzically. "Yeah, what's wrong with you? What happened?"

I shrugged. "Oh, just more of the usual. But I do need to talk to you." I turned to Ralph. "It seems like I'm always doing this to you."

"Oh, please, don't give it a second thought. I have an early-morning meeting tomorrow anyway. This just gives me an excuse to get to bed before midnight." He leaned over and kissed Megan on the forehead, turned to hug me, and left.

"You are so lucky, Megan. He's a real sweetheart."

"He just asked if we could be exclusive," she said excitedly. "What do you think about that?"

"I couldn't be happier." I hugged her. "You did say yes, didn't you?"

"I did. Okay, enough about my life. Tell me what's wrong."

I hugged her and said, "Megan, I am so glad you're home. I really need a shoulder to cry on."

We yakked for hours about my dilemma. I told her about Mom's suggestion, and she loved the idea. She agreed it was a long shot, but it would definitely get Barry's attention.

This just had to work—I wouldn't have it any other way.

Chapter Nineteen

I left earlier than usual in the morning and headed straight to The Festive Masquerade, a costume shop close to the office. Fortunately, the owner was a friend of Mom's, who had his home number. He agreed to meet me at the shop before business hours.

I knocked on the door, and an older man opened it.

"Good morning, Cassie. Come in. We're all ready for you."

I extended my hand in greeting. "It's very nice to meet you, Mr. Brunello. I can't tell you how much I appreciate your opening the shop early."

"It's not a problem. Maybe you can tell your friends about us."

"I definitely will." I took a quick scan of the store. It

was loaded with every type of costume you could imagine. "May I see my costume?"

"Absolutely. And if it's not what you'd expected, or if you've changed your mind about which costume you want, we can do that too."

"Thank you."

"Rosemarie, will you please show Cassie her costume?" he said, raising his voice.

A woman in her mid-forties walked out from the back, chewing on the bagel she held in her hand.

She smiled when she saw me. "Hi, Cassie. It's so nice to meet Lucy Pirelli's daughter. We just love your mother at St. Mary's Women's Auxiliary. She's a real nice lady."

I was always surprised at the number of friends Mom had. I guess she didn't have as many problems with other people.

"Hi, Rosemarie. It's very kind of you to allow me to interrupt your breakfast."

She pulled a costume off the rack and showed it to me.

"This is perfect. Do you have a room where I can apply the makeup too?"

"Actually, I can apply the makeup for you. Once I'm finished, you can get dressed. Follow me."

Rosemarie applied my makeup, and I quickly changed into the outfit, laughing at my reflection in the mirror.

"You look terrific, Cassie. I'm sure you'll get a million laughs today."

I gathered the rest of my belongings and put them

into the sports bag I carried. All set to go, I paid Mr. Brunello and exited the store, then headed for the office. I was certain Barry would be sitting behind his desk, since he always enjoyed the early-morning hours before the other employees arrived. With my plan in place, I knew exactly what I had to do.

I took the elevator to the twentieth floor and carefully exited, struggling to maintain my balance in the floppy shoes I was wearing. When I approached his office door, my heart began to race, and the thought of turning back occurred to me. *Knock off the crap,* I told myself. *This is a golden opportunity, and I need to take it.*

I turned the corner, and without a moment's hesitation I barged right into his office. To my surprise, the officers of Merrill sat around his conference table.

Crap, I'd forgotten Thursday was his meeting day. I chastised myself. *Okay, just breathe—inhale, exhale, breathe. You're fine. You can do this.*

Everyone looked up when I entered. They were stunned, but no one could have been as stunned as I. They began to laugh.

Dan Rafferty was the first to speak. "Well, will you look at this? The guy gets a promotion, and he arranges entertainment for us this morning. Is this your way of saying good-bye?"

What? Barry got a promotion, and I didn't know a thing about it? Good-bye?

Barry stared at me, his frown questioning who the silly-looking clown was standing before him. I'd meant the costume to show him I knew I'd been a fool. Panic set in, and I turned to leave. One of my floppy shoes became tangled on the leg of a chair, and I began to fall. The cherry red nose I wore clipped the back of the chair and sailed through the air toward one of the officers, who cupped his hands as if he were catching a fly ball for the Mets.

I tried to break my fall but skidded into home plate—right in front of the office door. Barry jumped up. A look of recognition suddenly came over his face, and I pleaded with my eyes, begging him not to reveal my identity.

I had to hand it to the guy—he was able to read my expression even under the makeup. Without divulging my identity, he came to my rescue and helped me up.

Laughing, he announced, "Yeah, I thought you guys could use some loosening up this morning. Thank you, Clara Belle. That will be all."

Standing upright, I took a bow. Hey, I had to make them think it was staged. I exited the office, leaving behind a roar of laughter.

I took the elevator down to the lobby, which was now filled with employees. A crowd gathered by the door, laughing at me running toward the exit. I didn't wait around to hear what they were saying, because I needed to get out of the building as fast as I could. Fortunately, a cab pulled up in front of the building, and I jumped in as soon as the passengers exited. I gave my home address. The last thing I needed was for someone to recognize me.

The cabbie was amused by my attire. He laughed. "Early party, huh? It seems like I'm always picking up clowns."

"You are? So I guess this is commonplace in New York?"

"What kind of stunts do you do? Did you perform magic tricks?"

"Ah, no, I was just trying to get someone's attention."

"I bet you did, lady!"

"Oh, yeah. Big-time." I shook my head. "Yeah," I said, scrunching up my face, "big-time."

My heart rate slowed down by the time we reached my apartment building. The driver pulled up in front, and I reached into my pocket and paid the fare. I put the key in the door and released a sigh of relief once I was inside.

"Man, I'm such a butt-head."

I sat down on the sofa. I couldn't believe I'd screwed up again. A vision of Barry's stunned, handsome face flashed before my eyes.

I hoped the others didn't make my identity. Somehow I knew Barry would never reveal it.

I headed for the bedroom to undress and remove the makeup from my face. I still couldn't believe the news about his promotion and departure. Where was he going?

"I wonder when he was going to tell me. Or if he was going to tell me at all," I muttered.

The phone rang, and I picked it up without checking the caller ID first. With receiver in hand, I looked at the name and panicked.

I am so fired! I cried out in silent agony. *This will be his last duty before he leaves.* I quickly composed myself.

"Hi."

He laughed. "I can't believe you would go to such lengths to get my attention. Well, you've got it."

"Barry, let me . . . oh, hell, you don't want to hear it."

"Oh, but I do. Only, you know what? Stay right where you are. I'm on my way over to your place. Is Megan there?"

"No, I'm by myself."

"Good. I'll see you in a few minutes."

My heart was pounding. I didn't know what to expect. He didn't sound as if he was going to fire me, but maybe he was on his way over to tell me off. Had my plan worked? What would I do for an encore if it hadn't?

I rehearsed my lines a few times. I knew exactly what I wanted to say to him.

I finished dressing and waited for him to arrive. The doorbell rang, and I hesitantly walked over to it, apprehensive about what to expect. I opened the door, and Barry stood there smiling at me. He closed the door. We stood and stared into each other's eyes. His tender expression hit me full force. I tried to focus on what I wanted to say to him and began to speak. I needed to tell him what I was feeling.

"Congratulations. Where are you going?" I said instead.

"I've taken a job with one of our subsidiaries in Los Angeles."

Maybe he'll ask me to go with him once I tell him how I feel. Oh, Lord, please let him ask me.

I smiled. "I'm . . . very happy for you. Please, come and sit down. We have a lot to talk about."

He stopped in his tracks and looked at me questioningly. "What do you want to talk about?"

I bit my lip and said, "Let's sit down."

"Okay," he said cautiously.

"I dressed up like a clown today and went to your office—I should say, charged into your office, making an absolute ass of myself—because I'd come to a turning point in my life that I wanted to share with you. And I wanted your undivided attention. Although my actions were rather over the top, I was feeling pretty giddy. So I took a chance, because it was one I had to take. The important thing right now is I *do* have your attention, and I can tell you face-to-face how much you mean to me."

He held up a hand for me to stop.

"No, please don't stop me now. I need to get this off my chest . . . and you need to know how I feel about you."

He smiled while I continued to steamroll him.

"Since you hired Michael, I realized I was being overly ambitious for all the wrong reasons. The other night, when I called you at home, I could hear a female voice in the background. The thought of you being with another woman . . . I was jealous. I was afraid that you'd moved on, and I was afraid I'd never have another chance to show you—"

He cut me off in midsentence. "Please, Cassie, do—"

I silenced him with a hand and continued to spill my guts. "I need you to know why my career was so important to me. I needed to prove to my mother that I was capable of success. She's been such a controlling influence in my life, the need for recognition became an obsession, just so I could prove her wrong."

I licked my lips, because my mouth felt as though it were full of cotton balls.

"I was distraught and like a zombie—until I finally had a long talk with my mother and realized what was really important to me. You know what that was?"

He didn't move. He continued to stare at me.

I smiled confidently, feeling liberated from my hang-up. "The most important thing to me is you." I smiled. "There, I said it. I finally said it."

He remained silent.

"So, do you think you would be content to date and see where it takes us? I know it would be long-distance now, but I'm willing to do that to have you in my life. What do you think? No commitments, just fun and laughter for now—get reacquainted all over again?"

He shook his head and remained silent for what seemed like an eternity. "Why couldn't you have said these things to me a few months ago?"

"Well, because I was blindsided by ambition. But I'm not anymore."

"I'm afraid you're too late." He shifted his weight. "My former fiancée and I have rekindled our relationship."

I felt as though I'd been clobbered over the head with a baseball bat. I remained motionless as he continued.

"When I first realized how I felt about you, I was willing to do almost anything to have you." His expression changed to a somber one. "After our trip to Dallas, I wanted you even more . . . so much so that I was willing to give up my job. But after your reaction, my pride stopped me from coming after you. With each day it became increasingly hard to deal with, so I hired Michael, because I couldn't handle being so close to you anymore. I wanted you in my arms, but you'd rejected me, and I wasn't willing to take that chance again."

My heart was pounding so rapidly, I thought it would burst through my chest. I was stunned beyond words. I'd screwed up my chance at true happiness, and now I was paying the price.

He looked at me as if he read my thoughts. "If you'd given me the slightest hint there was a chance you felt something for me, I probably never would have moved on."

Tears spilled down my cheeks. I was momentarily speechless. I swallowed hard and tried to put on a brave front before I opened my mouth to say something.

"Oh, Barry, I am so sorry. I should have stopped talking when you told me to."

"I'm sorry too, Cassie."

Chapter Twenty

I leaned against the door and listened to Barry's footsteps for as long as I could hear them. Tears streamed down my cheeks like a dam spilling over. I wanted to call my mother for comfort, but I couldn't muster up the strength. Instead, I went to my room and lay on my bed. I closed my eyes—and woke to the sound of Megan's voice. I sat up in bed, still groggy. I must have been sleeping for hours, because it was dark in the room. She flipped on the light, took one look at my face, and knew instantly what had happened. She sat down on the bed. She held me in an embrace for a long time while I sobbed.

"It's okay. Don't cry."

"I really messed up this time, Meg."

"I know it feels that way now, but it'll be okay. Go

ahead and cry all you want. I promise you'll feel better soon."

"I don't think so. I don't think I'll ever feel this way about another man. I just know I won't."

"That's not true. Remember how sad and depressed I was when Joey and I broke up? I thought the world was coming to an end. And look at me today."

I did remember what she went through. Having her remind me helped, and I stopped crying.

Megan wiped the tears off my cheeks. "Okay, I know what you need. Up and at 'em. We're going out on the town tonight."

"Oh, I don't think so. I just want to stay here and die."

"What?" she said. "Don't be ridiculous. You most certainly can go out, and you will. Remember, this is what you did for me, and today I'm very glad you did." She grabbed my legs and swung them over the side of the bed. "C'mon, girl, you can do this."

"But I really don't want to do this."

"I know you don't, but you have to. It's like having a car accident. If you don't get back behind the wheel, you'll never drive again." She stood staring at me with her hands on her hips. "Okay, I'm going to turn on the shower while you convince yourself that I'm not letting you off the hook."

With a springy bounce, she left and headed to the bathroom. I lay back down, closed my eyes, and begged sleep to take me away. No such luck. I could hear her footsteps shuffling back my way.

"I'm coming back into the room," she said melodically, her giggle echoing from the hallway.

"Gee, what a funny face you're making," she observed. "I wouldn't do that if I were you. You wouldn't want it to freeze that way, now, would you?" Her voice took on a firm tone. She pointed a finger at me. "Now, get into an upright position this minute, young lady, and get your butt outta that bed."

"Yeah, yeah, yeah."

As often as I give her a hard time, I know just how fortunate I am to have her as a friend. I don't know what I'd do without her. She's the one person in the world who can make me forget my troubles, at least for a while.

"Thanks, I needed that. I love you, Megan."

"I love you too." She thrust her finger forward. "Now get into that shower."

"Yes, ma'am."

When I finished, I walked into the living room, where Megan was waiting. "Hey, aren't you supposed to see Ralph tonight?"

"Yep, I was, but I think he can survive a night without me. I told him to go out with his friends. You have top billing tonight," she said with a smile.

While we were heading to the bar, I thought of Jason and asked, "Meg, does Ralph know about Jason and me?"

"What?" she said with raised eyebrows. "That you only want to be friends with him?"

"Yes."

"He does, but he said you shouldn't count on Jason's giving up that easily."

"Well, at least someone loves me."

"Are you kidding me? You have so many guys in love with you, I'm jealous."

"You are?"

"Nah. I just said that to make you feel better. But Jason is pretty serious about you, as is Sammy, even though you don't want to admit it."

"Oh, please. Sammy's delusional. Let's not even go there."

She looked at me. "I don't want to make you cry again, but maybe now that Barry is out of the picture, you'll feel different toward Jason. He is crazy about you . . . you know?"

I agreed. "He really is a wonderful man, but I don't want to think about him right now."

"That's cool."

Under the streetlight, I grabbed her arm and tossed my head back. "Hey, are my eyes still puffy?"

"Hmm," she said as she examined my face. "Just a tad, but if anyone asks, tell them you have allergies."

"Boy, you amaze me. You always have an answer."

She chuckled. "That's what I'm here for."

We entered Randazzo's Bar and Grill. Although we hadn't been there in a long time, it was nice to see some familiar faces. The band was cranking so loudly, all we could do was nod or wave hello to our friends. We stayed at the bar until closing.

When we got back to the apartment, I entered my bedroom and flopped down without removing my clothes. I think I might have been asleep before my head hit the pillow.

I didn't wake until I smelled the rich aroma of coffee. As soon as I picked my head up, I suddenly remembered I had a job, and the clock on the wall said ten. I ran to the kitchen. Megan gave me one of those quizzical looks.

"Oh, no," I shouted, "I'm late for work!"

"Relax, Cass. It's Saturday."

My hands went up to my aching head, "Oh, thank you, sweet Jesus." I slowly turned around and staggered back to bed, where I slept until the phone rang. I reached for it.

"Hi, sweetheart," Mom said.

"Hi, Mom," I said in a groggy voice.

"Oh, I'm sorry. I thought you'd be up by now." Her voice changed to a sympathetic tone. "I called earlier and spoke to Megan. She told me. I'm sorry things didn't work out for you."

I was still fascinated by this recent change in my mother. Who knew that the problems we'd had over the years all stemmed from my lack of attention to her, my acting as if I no longer needed her? Now that we were acting like mother and daughter again, I wanted to keep it that way.

"I'm sorry I didn't call you sooner, but I just didn't want to talk about it yet. I'm glad Megan told you."

"I am too. Would you like me to come over?"

"No, I'm okay now. Megan and I went out last night and got in very late. I guess that's why I've been sleeping all day. I needed to forget the mistake of the century."

"Oh, don't say that. There are reasons for everything."

This was coming from my mother? How neat is that? It was going to be hard getting used this new woman. Nevertheless, I liked it.

"Are you sure you don't want me to come over? I can be there in a flash."

"No thanks, Mom. But I will be there for dinner tomorrow. Maybe we can find some time away from the family so we can talk about what happened."

"I'd like that," she said in a gratified tone. "Why don't you come earlier than everyone else, so we can talk without interruption?"

"That's a great idea. I'll be there sometime around eleven so we have plenty of time before the rest of the clan arrives."

"That's wonderful. Okay, I'll let you get back to whatever you're going to do." I could hear the excitement in her voice. "I'm looking forward to seeing you tomorrow."

Chapter Twenty-one

The visit with Mom was like a breath of fresh air for a change, and I was feeling much better knowing I had her support. It was really nice to be with the family—even Aunt Mary.

During the ride back to my apartment, thoughts of Jason crossed my mind, and I suddenly realized I hadn't heard from him. "I guess I can't blame him," I said aloud.

An uneasy feeling welled in the pit of my stomach. Was I making another mistake? Maybe he'd decided to ditch the idea of trying to win me over after all. I'd been pretty self-absorbed these days—who could blame him? I didn't understand why I was even thinking about Jason that way. I guess I was more depressed than I imagined. But he was the one who'd said he wasn't giving up easily. I twisted my hair around a finger, a habit I'd broken a long time ago.

I'd been feeling insecure after what happened with Barry, and now that I hadn't heard from Jason, I was feeling put out about it. That made no sense, but I guess that's what I was doing. Somehow I'd lost sight of the people I cared most about in my attempt to achieve my career goals.

I ran up the stairs to my apartment. I checked to see if I had any messages, and there was one, but not from Jason. The message was from Sammy.

"Can you believe the audacity of this guy?" I muttered.

Even though he was the last person in the world I wanted to hear from, I suppose I had to give him credit for being persistent. At least it was a boost to my injured ego. I called out to Megan.

"Hey, Meg, are you here?"

When she didn't respond, I meandered into the kitchen and opened the refrigerator to find something to eat. The odor that escaped almost knocked me over.

"Whoa, I guess we haven't cleaned this thing out in a while." I began to check through the containers. "Oh, man, we could start our own medical lab with all the penicillin growing in here." I pulled every item out, one by one, and tossed them into the garbage. Housekeeping isn't my forte, but during times like these it can be therapeutic. I was scrubbing the interior of the refrigerator, my hands deep in suds, when I heard Megan.

"I'm in here, Meg." I turned to face her when she giggled.

"What on earth are you doing, Susie Homemaker?" She chuckled again. "Oh, wait, I get it. This is one of those therapy sessions, huh?"

"Yeah, well, you know me."

"Is it working?"

"Yeah, I guess so. I'm so engrossed in cleaning, I haven't thought about chocolate or how hungry I felt when I walked into the apartment."

She sniffed the air. "Ooh, what is that awful smell?"

I pointed to the inside of the refrigerator. "I think it was leftover pasta. I really wasn't able to identify it, but I think that's what it was." I shuddered, remembering what the contents of the container had looked like. "We had our very own lab growing in here."

"Oh, yuck! Do we have any bathroom spray?"

"Look in the linen closet."

She walked down the hall. "Oh, crap, we're out of spray!" she called from the hallway. "I'll open the windows. I don't want to smell that putrid odor all night."

"Why don't you take out the trash? That ought to get rid of the smell."

"Oh, yeah, I guess that would help, huh?" She grabbed the bag, started to walk toward the door, and then stopped. "Hmm, isn't this interesting?"

I turned to look at her. "What? What's so interesting?"

She started the laugh. "You. You're the one who's

always saying you don't want to get married, yet you look pretty domesticated to me with that apron on and that handkerchief tied around your hair. You fit the housewife image perfectly."

I chuckled. "Hey, don't get carried away with the image. That's from years of study at the Lucy Pirelli Good Housekeeping Academy."

She looked at me. "How could I have forgotten that?" She picked up the garbage bag and held it at arm's length, as though she was afraid something would eat through the plastic and attack her. "So does this mean you haven't eaten yet?"

"Nope, I haven't eaten yet. But I'm not so sure I want to eat anything ever again."

"Aw, c'mon. Let's go grab a bite at Morelli's."

"Not Morelli's. After seeing that container of pasta, or whatever it was, I don't want Italian food for at least a few days." I closed the door of the refrigerator. "Give me a minute. I need to take a fast shower."

We entered Logan's Bar and Grill. After we were seated and had ordered our drinks, I began thinking about Jason again.

"Okay, Cassie, you look like you want to ask me something."

"You know me too well."

"Well, that'll happen when you're friends with someone since kindergarten." She grinned. "So what's on your mind?"

"Okay. How's Jason? I haven't heard anything from him in a few days. I guess he's busy, huh?"

"Well, that he is."

"How do you know that?" I asked.

"Hmm." She shifted with unease. "Well, Ralph told me."

"Ralph told you what?"

"That Jason is busy." She looked away.

"Hey, I thought we were friends. You know something and won't tell me?"

"Because it's not my news to tell."

"Oh, I see. Can you at least tell me whether it's good or bad?"

"Well, it depends on how you look at it."

"Megan," I said abruptly, "what's going on with you?"

"Look, I promised I wouldn't say anything until Jason had an opportunity to tell you himself. Please go with the flow, and wait for him to call."

I gave her an annoyed shrug. "Okay, if that's the way it has to be." I sat back in silence.

"Oh, Cassie. You look just like your mother when she's mad." She knew that would stop me cold. "I think you'll be very happy for him. So stop with the silent treatment already."

The last thing I wanted was to reenact my mother's former behavior. That's why I love Megan. She tells it like it is.

"Okay, I'm sorry." I laughed. "That was a bit childish on my part. I respect your loyalty, so I'll stop asking and wait for his call."

"That's my girl. I'm sure he'll be calling you soon. And, speaking of calling, I promised Ralph I'd call him." She stood and walked away as she dialed his number on her cell phone.

I remained at the table and wondered what she knew about Jason and why I hadn't received a call. A few minutes later Megan was back at the table.

"So is everything going the way you wanted it to with Ralph?" I asked.

She gave me a big pumpkin smile, and I knew things were great.

"Wow! I guess things are going extremely well. Your face is lit up like a Christmas tree."

She rolled her eyes and shrugged, laughing with delight.

"Hmm. Well, are you going to fill me in?"

"Oh, there really isn't anything more than you already know. I'm just bouncing off the walls with excitement about having him in my life."

"Well, it doesn't get better than that, does it?"

"Nope, it doesn't. Except . . . maybe a proposal someday."

"Wow. Are things that serious?"

"I hope so. You know Valentine's Day isn't too far away. Maybe I'll get more than a box of chocolates."

"If that's what you want, then I'm in your corner, rooting him on."

We finished our meal and chatted about everything under the sun—that is, everything except Jason's news. After we finished eating, we headed back to the apartment.

Megan was especially happy the last half of the evening, and I couldn't understand why she was more excited now than she'd been before. We walked up the stairs to our apartment. Sitting in front of the door was a bouquet of red roses. My eyes lit up when I saw them. "I'll bet those are from Ralph. Boy, is he a romantic."

"Oh, you think so?"

"I do."

"Okay, then I'm going to go call him. Will you bring them into the house for me?"

"Sure. But why can't you call him inside?"

"That's okay. I have some free minutes left on my account that I'd like the cell company to pay for."

I shrugged. "Okay, suit yourself."

Megan walked back down the stairs. I shuffled through my handbag for my keys and was surprised when I felt a hand on my shoulder. I gasped and turned around, only to find Jason standing behind me.

"Crap!" I yelled. "You scared the daylights out of me."

"I'm sorry. I didn't mean to do that." He looked at the roses in my hand. "So how do you like them?"

"How do I like what?"

"The roses."

I laughed. "Oh, these are beautiful. Ralph really knows how to win a girl's heart."

"Cass, those aren't Megan's. They're yours."

"Mine?" I asked quizzically. "I don't understand why you left them at the door if you're standing right here."

He grinned. "I know. Let's go inside, and I'll explain. I have so much to tell you."

"Okay." I was a bit bewildered but happy I didn't have to wait any longer to hear what was going on. We entered and walked to the sofa. Jason took the bouquet, laid it on the sofa, then grabbed my shoulders and turned me around to face him. "I'm about to share the most exciting news of my life with you."

"Tell me. I'm dying to know what's going on. Everyone seems so mysterious these days."

"Cassie, do you know how much I love you?"

I didn't respond. "Tell me your news. I can't stand all this mystery."

"Okay. Brace yourself." He released me, and I sat on the sofa. "I've just been promoted. I'm going to be your new boss, Cass." He was grinning from ear to ear.

A flicker of apprehension coursed through me. I stuttered. "You . . . you are?"

"You look shocked."

"Well, I am a little. I really thought Ryan would be the one to replace Barry." Realizing how my comment sounded, I added, "Not that I don't think you're worthy of the promotion. I'm just surprised, that's all."

"Actually, I was too. I know Ryan's the fair-haired boy, and I didn't think I stood a chance, but Dan Rafferty called me into his office a few days ago and offered me the position."

"That's super! Congratulations. You'll make a wonderful VP."

"I'm planning on it. I have so many ideas about changes I want to make in the department."

"Jason? You do realize we can no longer hang out together, don't you?"

"That may be partly true. But I have a much better idea."

He had a devious smile on his face, causing me to wonder what he had up his sleeve. In an instant he was down on one knee.

I began to hyperventilate. *Oh, no. Please don't.*

Cripes, my life just keeps getting better and better all the time . . . it's like a freakin' soap opera.

Jason looked deeply into my eyes as he rubbed the top of my hand with his thumb.

"Cassie, I'm in love with you. I know you said you only wanted to be friends, but we *are* friends. That's the foundation for any successful relationship, and I feel very fortunate to have found you."

"Jason, don't." I held a hand up like a traffic cop. "Please don't say it."

"Don't say what? That I want you to be my soul mate forever—that I want to spend the rest of my life with you?"

"Oh, darn it," I said. "Now, why did you have to go and ruin it? You know how I feel. Besides, if you think that making me your wife is going to solve the problem, you'd better think again. I still can't work for you."

"I know, but you wouldn't have to work. My salary would be more than enough for a glamorous lifestyle. I'd be able to support you and a family very comfortably."

Shocked, I said, "Whoa, my friend. You'd want me to quit working?" With hands on hips, I said, "Are you out of your mind? When I leave Merrill, it will be because I want to, not because someone tells me I have to—that is, unless I'm fired for some reason."

He nodded. "No, I'm not out of my mind. At least I didn't think so when I came up with this idea." He shifted uneasily. "But if you really feel the need to work, you could find something part-time that wouldn't interfere with raising a family."

My hand went up again. "Let's see if I've got this straight." I could feel my face getting hot, and my voice rose. "You're suggesting I give up my career goals to satisfy *your* desires?"

I drew in a deep breath, frustrated at his inability to understand my feelings. I'd been thinking about him, true, but I'd never seen this side of his personality before.

"Cassie. What's come over you?" He looked at me as if he'd said nothing wrong.

I shook my head in bafflement. Impatience made my voice even louder. "Jason, whatever possessed you to spring a proposal on me?"

He looked at me, and his eyes were bleak.

"Look, Jason. It's late, and I'm tired and grumpy right now. Thank you for the flowers."

"C'mon, Cassie, don't blow me off like this."

"I can't think straight anymore. I'm tired and overwhelmed about everything right now. I really can't discuss this anymore. I need some rest."

Slowly he straightened up. "I'm not rushing you, but will you at least think about my proposal?"

I touched his arm to let him know I cared about him and his feelings. And I did. But not the way he needed me to. "Jason, you have become a very dear friend, but I'm afraid the way I feel about you will never be the way you'd like me to feel. I'm flattered you care about me. Really, I am, because I think you're a wonderful man, and I just know there's a wonderful woman out there worthy of your love."

His shoulders slumped in defeat. "I guess it was worth a shot." He looked up, a sincere expression on his face. "You sure there's no way I can convince you otherwise?"

"I'm sorry, but I'm afraid not." I thought about our conversation for a moment. "Please allow me to give you some sisterly advice, though. During your next proposal, make sure your intended wants all the same things you do before you tell her what she wants."

He smiled and leaned in to hug me. "You're right. Next time I decide to propose to someone, I'll make sure I run it by you first." His brows knit together. "Hey, wait a minute. Does that mean if I'd proposed the proper way, you would have said yes?"

I gave him a poke in the arm. "Jason!"

I walked him to the door and opened it. "I need to get some rest now. I'm very happy about your promotion— I think you'll make a wonderful vice president. Merrill is very fortunate to have you."

"What's going to happen with you now?"

"I'm not sure, but I'll think about my options over the weekend."

He planted a light kiss on my cheek. "Good night, Cassie. I'll see you Monday."

"Okay. Good night." I closed the door, walked into the kitchen, poured myself a glass of soda, then headed to my bedroom. I placed my glass on the nightstand and sat holding my head in my hands, still in a daze at the sequence of events.

"Wow, when is this ever going to stop?" I pulled the covers back, adjusted the pillows to support my back, flopped down onto the bed, and grabbed my drink. I re-capped my conversation with Jason. "I can't believe he asked me to marry him." I stopped talking to myself when my bedroom door opened.

"Hey, Cass, how'd it go?"

"Megan, did you know this was going to happen to-night?"

"Yes, I did," she said with a sheepish grin on her face.

"You of all people knew how I felt about Jason. Why didn't you tell him it was a bad idea?"

"That's unfair, Cassie," she said, pointing a finger at me. "Listen to what you're saying. My telling Jason to back off isn't something that should have come from me. What if you had changed your mind about the way you felt, and I ruined it before he ever asked you? You'd never have forgiven me."

"I know." I nodded. "You're right. As usual, I'm sorry I'm taking my anger out on you tonight." My eyes filled with tears. Megan gave me one of those sad, puppy dog looks, and I began to cry.

She came over to the side of the bed and held me while she patted my back. "It'll be okay. Why don't you consider taking some time off? You really need a break."

I dried my tears. "Maybe I do need to get away to think about everything that's happened. Unfortunately, I don't have any vacation time. I have five personal days left, but that's about it."

She nodded. "So take them. Trying to handle all this at once is pretty tough. Do you want me to take time off and go with you?"

"No. Actually, Megan, I think I need to do this one by myself. Thanks for the offer, though."

"You're right." She gave me a smile. "Going by yourself is probably a much better idea. It'll give you time to make your own decisions without any outside influence." She turned to walk out, then stopped. "I'm proud of you, Cassie. Sleep tight."

"Thanks, Meg. Would you mind switching off the light on your way out?"

"Sure. See you in the morning."

I lay there for several hours, thinking about Barry and Jason.

Somewhere in the midst of my thoughts I fell fast asleep and didn't wake until the sunlight was in my eyes. I sat up quickly, with an ache in the pit of my stomach, knowing I had several decisions requiring my attention. I walked to the closet, removed my robe from the hook on the back of the door, and slipped into it. I needed a cup of coffee.

I could see a note on the refrigerator when I entered the kitchen. Megan wanted me to know her where-abouts and asked me to call her when I woke up. I poured myself a cup of coffee left in the pot and placed it in the microwave to heat it up. The phone rang, and I hesitantly walked over to answer it.

"Hello?"

"Good morning, honey."

"Hi, Mom."

"How are you after all that's happened?"

"Megan called you?"

"Yes, she did. Don't be mad at her. She's really con-cerned about you."

"I'm not mad. I'm happy she called you—now I don't have to go through the whole thing again."

"Have you decided what you're going to do yet?"

"The only thing I have decided is to hibernate for a while to think things through."

"I agree you need to think things through, but I don't like the sounds of that hibernating stuff."

"Don't worry, Mom. I'll be okay. Please just bear with me for a while.

"Okay, I can do that. But I'm not going to let you get yourself into a state of depression either."

"I promise . . . I won't. Knowing you're there to listen is all I need right now. I'd like to rest. Can I call you later?" I started to cry.

"Aw, Cassie, I'm sorry you're so upset. You sure I can't do anything for you?"

"No thanks," I said through my tears, "but I appreciate the offer. I think I need to deal with this by myself. I'll catch up with you later."

"Okay. Do you want to come for dinner tonight? The whole family will be here."

"I can't. Please don't be upset, but I need some alone time. You understand, don't you?"

"Of course I do. Okay, honey. I'll be thinking about you. I love you."

"Thanks, Mom. I love you too." I hung up the phone and dried my tears with a tissue I found stuffed in the pocket of my robe, then picked up my cup and headed for the sofa. I turned on the television to temporarily distract me, but after a few minutes I became restless and decided I needed some chocolate.

On my way back into the kitchen I remembered we didn't have any chocolate, but I thought I'd check anyway, just in case. The sadness I was feeling called for the heavy artillery, and I was going after it. I remembered vowing I'd never touch the stuff again, but since I'd already cheated and nothing had happened, like being struck by lightning, I figured He understood and gave me a free pass.

I opened the cupboard and searched around with my hands. I couldn't see if there was anything on the top shelf—being short has its disadvantages—so I pulled a chair over to stand on. That's when I saw it—a huge box of chocolate turtles I'd forgotten about, tucked way back in a corner of the shelf. "Yippee!" I cried with delight. "Help is on the way."

I got down off the chair, clutching the box as if it were gold, and rushed back to the sofa, peeling the wrapper off along the way. "Eat as much chocolate as you want," I said to myself. "It's okay this time." I looked up to the ceiling and begged for mercy. "God, please don't be mad. You know I need this, right?" He didn't answer, but I pictured Him smiling down at me. I lifted the lid and looked at the white-spotted turtles. They'd been on the shelf a long time. I picked one up and smelled it. It smelled okay, so I popped it into my mouth. It tasted pretty stale, but I didn't care.

When I finished the last piece, I sat and waited for the chocolate to do its thing. A half hour later, I was still waiting. The only thing I felt was stuffed and bloated. "Maybe this is His way of telling me chocolate isn't the cure-all."

I don't know how long I sat and waited, but it seemed like a long time. The phone rang, and I checked the caller ID. It was Jason, so I picked up the receiver.

"Hello?"

"Hello right back atcha. How are you today?"

"I'm okay, Jason. How are you?"

"Good." I could hear him inhale a deep breath. "Uh, I have a question I'd like to ask you."

"Oh, no. What now?"

"Relax. It's a simple question."

"Okay, what is it?"

"I was right about you and Barry, wasn't I?"

I swallowed hard and didn't respond right away, giving myself time to think before I answered. "Yes, Jason, you were right. Nothing happened between us, though. It was just wishful thinking on my part."

"So was mine. I should have paid closer attention to what you'd been saying. I let my ego get in the way and hoped my salesmanship skills could convince you otherwise. It was the excitement of the promotion, and wanting to share that with you, but what I had planned was a dumb idea. You stopped us both from making a big mistake, and I'm grateful to you for that. I mistook our friendship for love, but you were right. So don't beat up on yourself about refusing my offer. Okay?"

"Thank you for understanding, Jase. I never meant to hurt you."

"I was a little down about it at first, but after thinking it over, I knew you refused for all the right reasons. Are you okay? You really sound down."

"Actually, I'm feeling a bit numb . . . as though I'm having an out-of-body experience."

"And my putting more pressure on you didn't help. Why don't you take some time off?"

"I only have five personal days. I don't think a week off is going to help the state I'm in."

"Okay, well, here's what I can do as your new boss. I'll discuss it with Rafferty and see what we can come up with."

"Oh, I'm not sure Rafferty will go along with it. He doesn't like me very much."

"Who told you that?"

"Well, I guess I just assumed that since he didn't like Barry very much, he didn't care for me either."

"We had a conversation a few days ago about you. He has a very high regard for your work and dedication."

"He does?"

"He most definitely does. He said Barry told him you were responsible for the rush of customers after the Dallas conference. You're a star in his eyes."

"Oh, wow! But you're not going to tell him the truth about why I need time off, are you?"

"Of course not. I'll just say you need to take care of some family matters. He doesn't need to know the details."

"Thank you, Jason. That's so nice of you."

"I'll call him at home and get back to you. Oh, one of the things he did mention during our conversation when he offered me the promotion was our close relationship, so when you return, we may need to give you another job, but don't think about it now. You know I'll take care of you."

"Wow, Jason, you've brought some sunshine into an otherwise bleak day."

"Hey, I aim to please. All right, let me call him. I'll get back to you."

"You're an amazing friend, Jason. Thank you."

"You too, Cassie. Okay, I need to hit the shower."

I returned to the sofa and watched television for the remainder of the day. Except for Jason's next call, offering me three weeks off, and a few bathroom breaks, I never took my eyes off the screen until Megan walked in.

"Hey, how are you doing today? Are you feeling any better?"

"I'm okay now that I've just finished off the entire box of spotted turtles."

"Spotted turtles?"

"Yep. They were stale, but I didn't care."

"I thought you made a vow to give up chocolate."

"I did, but He understood," I said, pointing toward heaven. "Actually, now that I think about it, He did respond to me."

"Oh, yeah? How's that? Personally I think you've had too much chocolate, and you're losing it. You're sounding really irrational." She came over and felt my forehead.

I laughed, removing her hand. "Megan, stop. I'm fine . . . honest." She frowned. I giggled. "Before I ate the turtles, I apologized to Him for breaking the vow. He responded by having Jason call me. See how that works?"

"Okay." She kept looking at me as if I was losing it. "So what did Jason say?"

"We had a long conversation. He thanked me for refusing his offer and apologized for not seeing the handwriting on the wall."

"He said all that?" Megan's eyes were wide with surprise.

"Yes." I nodded. "So now we're good. No hard feelings at all."

"That must be relief to you."

"It is a relief. Then we discussed my taking time off, and he called Rafferty, who gave his approval."

"That's surprising. I thought you said Rafferty didn't like you."

"That's what I thought, but apparently Barry put in a good word for me."

"Well, isn't that special," Megan said sarcastically. "That was the least he could do after what happened."

"Oh, I'm not mad at him. I'm just sad."

"I know. But I promise it will get better. Honest, it will."

"Where are you off to tonight?"

"Nowhere. I'm staying right here with you. Ralph is off deep-sea fishing with some friends, and I thought this was a good opportunity for us to have a girlfriend weekend. What do you say?"

"I'm not very good company right now. I'd like to stay here and sulk for a while."

"I don't like the sound of that very much." She frowned. "Look, sweetie, I know you're upset, but you can't let this ruin the rest of your life."

"I'm not, but I just need time to think. Right now everything seems to be a major production for me."

"What Jason did today was very nice, but let's not use that as an excuse to dwell on the self-pity crap, okay?"

"You know, you're beginning to sound like my mother."

"Well, if that's the advice Mama's giving you, then I don't mind sounding like her."

"Okay, I'm going to bed now."

"No, you're not. I ordered eggplant parmigiana for us, and it should be here any minute."

"Eggplant parmigiana? Oh, well, in that case . . ."

"Thought that would get your attention. Listen, on this Barry thing . . . so you made a mistake by falling in love with the wrong man. He made a mistake too. But he's not sulking. He's off to a new job with his girl-friend hanging off his arm."

"You're right. You always are. But it doesn't make me feel any better."

"Look, turn that sadness into anger. Get mad. Get

madder than hell at him. That will stop those bad feelings. Shall I get the pillows?"

I giggled. "No. I don't think I have the energy to wallop you."

The doorbell rang. Megan stood and walked to the door. "Our dinner has arrived."

We finished eating, and I rubbed my stomach. "I'm not feeling very well right now. I think I'm going to lie down for a while."

Megan walked down the hall to the medicine cabinet and returned. "Here, take these antacids. Get your shoes on, and we'll take a stroll. The fresh air ought to make you feel better."

"I don't want to."

Megan's face turned beet red. "And I don't care. Stop your whining, and get your shoes on. We're going for a stroll."

"Megan, I know you're trying to help me, but you're beginning to annoy the heck out of me."

"Good, that's exactly what I want to do. Now get your shoes on."

Chapter Twenty-two

The first week passed quickly. I hadn't done anything noteworthy, hadn't called anyone, had ignored Megan's attempts to help, and had continued to sulk. Thursday evening, Megan and Mom both walked in the door. I was still in my pajamas. Shocked, Mom gave me the infamous "Mom" look and began to speak.

"Okay, Cassie, a week is more than enough time to sulk. Megan and I have stood by and allowed you to, but this is it. You're finished sulking. Get to the shower, and get dressed. We're going out."

I began to open my mouth to speak, and she interrupted me while Megan looked on with a smile on her face. She pointed a finger at me. "Not a word—do you hear me?"

Feeling like a child again, I defended myself. "I

wasn't going to say anything, except you're right. Okay, I'm heading to the shower now."

"Good. We'll be waiting."

I walked down the hall and could swear I heard Megan and Mom chuckling. I actually snickered under my breath too. I hadn't seen Mom that angry in a long time. She was right, though, a week was long enough. I still had two weeks left, and I was going to make the most of them.

I stepped into the shower and scrubbed my hair and body. When I was done, I dressed in jeans and a shirt and entered the living room, where Mom and Megan waited for me.

"Megan," Mom said, "who is this girl? Do you know her?"

I responded. "That bad, huh?"

They both answered simultaneously, nodding their heads in agreement. "Uh-huh."

I walked over and hugged each of them. "Thanks for being there for me. I love both of you very much."

"Nice to have you back among the living," Megan said.

"Thanks. It's nice to be back." I looped my arms though theirs, and we walked out to the car. "Where are we going?"

"We're not telling."

I rose early on Friday morning, before Megan was up, and surprised her with a pancake breakfast. She walked into the kitchen.

"Mmm, what's that glorious smell?"

"I smiled. "I've made you a thank-you breakfast of sausage and pancakes. Please have a seat at the table while I bring you your coffee."

She sat down and placed the cloth napkin on her lap. "My, my, you're certainly the domestic diva this morning. Last night was fun, wasn't it?"

"It was a wonderful evening. I was surprised my mother would go to Chippendale's, weren't you?"

"To say the least. She's a hoot, Cassie. I couldn't believe it when she tucked the five-dollar bill into that guy's G-string."

"I know. My father would die if he knew. She was like one of the gang last night." I smiled. "I'm so glad Mom and I straightened things out between us. She's really quite nice, you know?"

Megan nodded. "You're right, she is."

I poured our coffee, went back to the counter for her plate, and placed it in front of her.

"Oh, wow, Cassie, I never knew you had such talent. You take after your mother when it comes to cooking." She eyed the plate favorably. "Wow, look at this presentation. Fruit next to the pancakes, hot syrup, and butter on the side. You could be a chef, you know?"

I giggled. "Okay, don't get carried away here."

"So what's on your agenda for today?"

"I'm actually going to call your friend Rosie, the travel agent, and see what she can come up with for the two weeks I have left. I still have some issues I need to work through, and being alone on some island might do just the trick. What do you think?"

"I think that's the best idea you've had." She cut her pancake and put a bite of it into her mouth. "Oh, yum, these are delicious. Wow, Cass, I'm impressed."

After she finished eating, she reapplied her lipstick, picked up her briefcase, and walked over to hug me. "Thank you for such a nice treat this morning. I'm really proud of you." She opened the front door and stopped. "Hey, do you need Rosie's number?"

"I can look it up. I'll call you after my plans are made. Have a super day." I closed the door and walked back into the kitchen to begin cleaning up the dishes. Afterward, I found Rosie's number in the phone directory and dialed it. She wasn't there, but I left a message telling her what I wanted, and asked her to return my call. I poured myself another cup of coffee and continued to clean the apartment, waiting for Rosie's call. While I vacuumed, I actually began feeling the excitement of knowing I was going away. I checked the caller ID when the phone rang and saw *Vincent Travel Agency* on the screen.

I picked up the receiver. "That was fast."

"Hey, Cassie. Yes, it's me," Rosie said. "I didn't know exactly what you were looking for, but I came up with a few things. Tell me how much time you have."

"Two weeks."

"That's terrific, because I found something phenomenal that you're going to love."

"Great. Where am I going, and how soon can I leave?"

"It depends on how fast you can pack. I have a flight leaving at six-thirty tomorrow morning to San Diego. Then a representative will meet you at the airport and drive you to the port, where you'll meet the ship."

"Meet the ship? What are you talking about?"

"You are going on a singles cruise. It's loaded with things to do. You only have to unpack once, and the ship takes you everywhere you need to go. By the way, bring a costume for the grand mystery ball."

"Ooh, that sounds like fun. Okay, I'll take it."

"Great. Stop by the office this afternoon about two for your tickets."

Excited, I said, "I better get busy packing. I'll see you later. Thanks, Rosie."

"You bet."

"I'm so excited," I said, dancing around the room. "Finally, something positive is happening in my life." I picked up the phone and dialed The Festive Masquerade, ordered a costume, and scheduled a time to stop and pick it up. I called Mom to invite her to lunch, and then pulled my luggage out of the closet to begin packing.

Chapter Twenty-three

I exited the plane and headed to the baggage claim area to retrieve my luggage. The airport was buzzing as people waited at each of the carousels to seize their luggage and get on with their plans. I was happy when my suitcase sputtered out of the large mouth of the carousel and dropped down onto the moving belt. I struggled to yank it off the belt, when suddenly a man approached and offered his assistance.

"Here, why don't you let me get this for you?" His dark eyes flashed with determination. "Are you going on the singles cruise?"

"Yes, but how did you know?"

"I saw you reading the sign the Utopia Cruise Line's representative was holding, so I assumed you were going." His laugh was pleasant, giving me a warm feeling about him.

"That I am. I assume you are too?"

"Yes." He extended his hand. "Allow me to introduce myself. My name is Josh Barnett."

"Hello, Josh Barnett. I'm Cassie Pirelli."

We joined the other passengers waiting in line. Carl, the cruise line's representative, interrupted our conversation.

"Welcome to San Diego. We are about to board the bus for a short ride to the port, where you'll be greeted by our friendly photographers ready to record the start of your thirteen glorious days of food, fun, and laughter. Be prepared to party the entire time. We have a lot of fun things planned for you." He laughed when everyone cheered. "Hey, you all brought your costumes for tonight's masquerade party, didn't you?"

Everyone was bursting with excitement as they acknowledged that they had indeed packed their costumes.

"Great! Okay, please have your passports and tickets ready to show as you walk by. We will be taking bus number three, so allow me to lead the way."

I turned to Josh. "Have you ever been on a cruise before?"

"No. This is my first, but I have several friends who have taken this same cruise. How about you?"

"Nope. It's my first also."

"Well, good, we can learn together," he said with a wide grin.

Interesting, how this guy's already staked a claim.

I smiled back at him without responding. I was on this cruise to think, and that's what I was going to do. Well, I suppose I could have a little fun, but I wasn't so sure it was going to be with him. I found a seat, and Josh plopped himself right down next to me.

After the short ride from the airport, the bus stopped, and I looked in awe at the size of the ship. I had no idea I'd be floating on anything so huge.

"Hey, are you going to sit there all day, or are you going to get on that ship and start having some fun?" Josh's comment startled me, and I jumped.

"Sorry, I didn't mean to scare you."

I giggled. "That's okay. Will you look at the size of that ship?" I said. "I don't know what I was expecting, but this is really exciting."

"Well, then, let's not dally."

We both walked into the reception area to show our tickets and obtain our ID's to board the ship. Once I was checked in, I was ready to walk the gangplank. Fortunately, Josh became enthralled with some other females, and I was able to enjoy the excitement of my first cruise all on my own without a tagalong. The photographers captured each passenger as we walked the plank. When it was my turn, the photographer said, "Okay, miss, smile pretty."

"Gee, I haven't combed my hair in a couple of hours. I can only imagine how great this picture is going to turn out."

"Yeah, but you wouldn't want to miss out on a record of your first few minutes, would you?"

"No, I guess not," I said, unconvinced.

The camera flashed, and I made my way onboard. The crew was hard at work sorting through a huge pile of suitcases and taking them to the appropriate cabins.

I checked the sign on the wall indicating in which hallway my cabin was located. I found my cabin, used my key card to unlock the door, and walked into the small but adequate room. It had a double bed in the center, two portholes, a television, and, best of all, a box of chocolates and a fruit and cheese platter. Perrier was being chilled in an ice bucket. A beautiful vase contained beautiful red roses. The card attached simply said, *Enjoy your cruise. You're in for a real treat.*

"Wow, Rosie really knows how to treat her customers. How nice is that?" My luggage hadn't arrived yet, so I sat on the sofa and looked out over the ocean through one of the portholes, drinking the Perrier and snacking on cheese. That only lasted a few minutes, though, because I was eager to walk around to see where everything was located. This cruise came about so quickly, I'd barely had time to realize just how amazing it was going to be.

I walked the decks, taking in the beauty of the décor. It was just a wonderful sight to see—a palace on water. I walked into the lounge and over to a group who had gathered in a corner, chatting excitedly. When I approached, one woman announced my arrival.

"Hi, please join us." She smiled. "My name is Ericka. What's yours?"

"I'm pleased to meet you, Ericka. I'm Cassie."

"What a great name. I'll bet you're a lot of fun."

I laughed. "Hmm . . . I suppose I can be."

"Well, that's good, because this group is all about fun, and we're ready to P-A-R-T-Y."

And that they were. One of the women noticed we were sailing, and we all ran to the windows to watch the ship leave port. Shortly after, I checked the time. "Hey, we have a masquerade party in about an hour." With that, the group disbanded, vowing to watch for each other.

When I reached my cabin, I was happy to see my luggage sitting there. I began putting my things away in the drawers and closet. Fortunately, my costume was in a garment bag provided by the store and wasn't wrinkled, since I'd carried it onboard the flight and was able to hang it in a closet.

I unzipped the bag and became excited about the prospect of having a *good* time dressed in a costume.

I pulled the gown out of the bag. It really was pretty, and I was glad I'd selected something manageable— Belle, from *Beauty and the Beast.* I wanted something low maintenance compared to the clown suit I'd worn a few weeks ago. Floppy shoes were not my forte.

I applied the final touches to the wig and placed the mask over my eyes. When I reached the lounge, the array of costumes presented a delightful sight.

Excitement welled inside me. Since we were all in costume, I really didn't have any idea who these people were, but it was okay with me. I was just happy to be there.

Based on what I'd experienced thus far, I was confident the cruise was going to be just the medicine I needed to mend my tattered heart and lift me from the sadness I felt.

Music played as several passengers danced and joked with one another. Looking around at the costumes, I was amazed at how elaborate some of them were. I laughed when I saw one of my shipmates dressed as Beast—the mate to my costume.

I giggled, walking up to him. I assumed it was a man because of the figure he cut. With my luck, it would be Josh Barnett. Nope. I was relieved when I heard a deep, muffled voice. He sounded almost like Marlon Brando in *The Godfather.*

"Would you like to dance?" he said.

"I'd love to, Beast. Thank you for asking."

He extended his hand, and we hit the dance floor and glided around like Fred and Ginger, attracting the attention of those around us.

"I think it's pretty amazing that you wore the partner to my costume. What made you decide on this particular one?"

"Oh, I don't know," he said. "I was in the costume shop and saw the mask and thought it would be fun." He chuckled. "It sure is making the evening lively, isn't it?"

"It certainly is." I looked around the dance floor. "Everyone is staring at us," I said with some embarrassment.

"That's probably because we're the best-looking couple here. Why, they might even crown us king and queen of the prom," he teased.

"This is so much fun. Thank you for being here and making this evening so special," I said.

Holy smokes! I can't believe I just said that to someone I just met. Then again, my mother has always told me that sometimes it only takes a short time to find someone you really enjoy being with.

"Thank you for being here too."

My heart fluttered. *I don't know what's happening here, but this guy is really charming.*

"Would you like to sit for a while, maybe have a drink or something?" I said.

"Well, I'd have to remove my mask to have a drink, and I don't want to reveal my identity until the appropriate time."

"Were you here this afternoon in the cocktail lounge?" I asked. "Your voice doesn't sound familiar."

"I didn't arrive until just before sailing."

"Oh, so I guess you didn't meet any of us, then. Aren't you just dying to know who everyone is?" I said excitedly.

"I am."

We danced for several more sets, laughing at each other's jokes and having a good time.

"You must be terribly thirsty. Why not take a drink into the men's room so you can remove your mask in there," I suggested. "That way you won't ruin the surprise."

He snapped his fingers. "Now, why didn't I think of that? See? That's just what we men need. A smart woman by our side."

I couldn't help but smile. "Thank you. That's a nice compliment." I picked up a drink from a waiter passing by and handed it to him. "Here, go ahead and enjoy a drink. I'll wait here for you. . . . I mean, if you want me to." Embarrassed by my comment, I said, "I'm sorry. I didn't mean to be so presumptuous."

He laughed. "You weren't. We've been together since the party began. If we weren't having fun, we would have gone our separate ways, don't you think?"

"Thanks. I guess you're right." I smiled. "Okay, go enjoy that drink."

I watched him walk away, and my heart filled with joy at the comfort I felt with this man. I was taken by his strong embrace while we were dancing, feeling as safe and secure in his arms as though I'd known him for years instead of hours.

He returned a short while later, snuck up behind me, and whispered in my ear, sending chills down my spine.

"Are you enjoying yourself, Belle?"

I laughed and played along. "Why, yes, Beast."

"I'm glad," he murmured. He pulled me back onto the dance floor, and we finished another set.

"Would you like to walk around the deck for a while?"

I curtsied. "I'd love to."

He held me around the waist and guided me out the door and onto the deck. I could feel the soft, warm wind blowing against my face. Except for the glow of a silvery moon and the lights outlining the ship, the darkness was almost surreal, as if I was in another world.

Beast reached for my hand, and I willingly accepted his invitation. I couldn't quite figure out what was happening to me, but I was feeling a strong connection to this man. Something I'd never felt before, not even with Barry.

I turned to him and gave him a warm smile. He squeezed my hand, and my heart skipped a beat.

Several passengers commented on our costumes as they walked by.

He laughed. "We certainly have created quite a stir."

"Yeah, I know. It really is interesting how we chose the same theme."

"When I was in the restroom before, one of the guys asked if you and I had planned this."

"What did you tell him?"

"I told him we'd just met onboard ship."

We continued to walk around the deck. The glide of the ship across the calm water was intoxicating, and it was easy to see why so many couples fell in love on cruises.

"Isn't this beautiful?" I said. "Look over there. Can you see the outline of that ship?"

"Oh, yeah, that is nice."

A passenger opened the door and announced that the unveiling was about to take place. The band was playing the theme song from "Love Boat."

"Oh, wow," I said with a nervous laugh. "Are you nervous?"

"Not at all. I'm looking forward to it." He squeezed my hand again. "Hey, will you excuse me? I need to use the restroom before the official unveiling."

Again I surprised myself. "Sure, but don't be gone too long."

"Okay, I'll be back in a flash." He left, and a costumed woman walked over to me.

"Aren't you that little brunet named Cassie?"

I recognized her voice and laughed. "I am indeed, Ericka."

"You're really hitting it off well with Beast. Do you know him?"

"No, I haven't a clue who he is. He's much taller than any of the men we met this afternoon. And he did say he arrived just before the ship sailed. Do you know who he is?"

"No, I don't, but I think it's quite a coincidence you two are characters from the same story. Are you sure you don't know him? You two look like you already have relationship of some sort."

"Purely coincidental, I assure you."

"So, tell me about him. You really looked as though you were enjoying his company."

"Mmm," I purred, "he's yummy. He's such a gentleman. He makes me feel safe and secure."

"Sounds like you might have a thing going on here with the masked man."

"Maybe so." Just thinking about it made my heart skip a beat. I was shocked that I could feel this way about a total stranger. Maybe it was the cruise, but being around him made me feel as though we'd known each other for years. I smelled the scent of his cologne on my hand, and a smile came across my face.

I watched the door, waiting for his return. When the announcement came for us to remove our masks, Beast was nowhere to be found. A wave of disappointment came over me, as if I'd just been flattened by a steamroller. I decided to call it a night and headed back to my cabin. I unlocked the door and found another vase of red roses. The card was signed, *Beast.*

"What the heck is going on here?" I said aloud. There was a knock on the door, and I thought it was a steward.

"Who is it?"

"It's me, Belle. Can you open the door?"

"Okay." I unlocked the door and let him in. "What happened to you?"

"I left because I didn't want to take off my mask in front of everyone."

"But, why? Are you afraid they won't like you?"

"Something like that. I didn't want you to embarrass me, and I thought it would be better if we were alone."

"I wouldn't have embarrassed you."

"Yes, I think you might have."

"Do you know me?"

He didn't respond.

"Do you want to remove your mask now?"

"I want to ask you something first. I know it's only been three hours, but I was wondering if you were feeling the same thing I've been feeling tonight."

"What, exactly, have you been feeling?"

"Like there is something really special going on between you and me."

I smiled. "I felt that too. Let's not waste any more time. On the count of three. Are you ready?"

"Yes. No, wait."

I laughed. "What are we waiting for?"

"May I kiss you first?"

"Okay. Sure."

"Well, you'll have to keep your eyes closed, because I have to remove my mask to do it."

"All right." I giggled with nervous anticipation. "I can do that."

"Do you promise you won't peek?"

"I promise. Honest."

I shut my eyes and leaned forward, waiting for his lips to brush mine. In an instant his arms held me tightly against him. His lips devoured my mouth with excitement. He released me.

I inhaled, trying to catch my breath. "Mmm. That was wonderful. May I open my eyes now?" I begged. "I can't stand this much longer."

"Okay. No, wait."

"What now?" I asked.

"May I remove your mask?" he asked.

"Sure, if you want to. I hope you're not disappointed."

"I hope you're not disappointed with me," he said.

He began removing my mask. Then held me at arm's length, and I could feel his eyes looking at me. "You're amazing."

I giggled, feeling like a schoolgirl. "Thank you. *Now* can I open my eyes?" I asked.

"I'm going to turn around so you'll see the back of my head." He laughed. "That way, if you're disappointed, I can make a mad dash for the door."

"You are too funny. Okay, turn around," I said impatiently. I opened my eyes, and something about his dark, wavy hair looked familiar. He slowly turned back to face me. I stood motionless, shocked with disbelief. I couldn't speak.

He took my hand in his. "Cassie Pirelli, I want you in my life," he said as he looked at me tenderly. "I'm afraid of what I'll miss if I don't. Please say you'll give us a chance."

I stuttered. "S-Sammy?" I had so many questions. "But—but—how did you know I'd be here?"

"Rosie . . . she's my cousin."

I was still in a state of shock.

He began to pace. "Look, when Rosie called to tell me you were taking this cruise and that there would be a costume ball the first night, I figured this was my one shot at convincing you that we were made for each other. I wanted you to get to know the real me, even if I had to hide behind a mask. Please don't blow me off this time."

I smiled at him. "I won't blow you off." I reached for his hand. "Nope," I said. "I'm actually going to give us a chance. Believe it or not, I've admired your perseverance. Even though I've never been very nice to you, you never gave up. That says a lot about who you are."

He smiled at me, and my heart skipped a few beats. At that very moment I realized that reaching my career goals was still important, but for the right reasons, not because I had to prove something to my mother. I smiled at him and walked right back into his arms, where I belonged.